SECRETS

CAN

KILL

BY

JOSEPH REDDEN

For Mom and Dad,

Thank you so much for your support on all my writing and photography projects. I would never have been able to do this without your help.

CHAPTER 1

The driver shook his fist and cussed out the man who almost slammed his motorcycle into his car when he sped around the bend.

"You moron!" screeched the motorist. "What the hell is wrong with you?"

The honking jarred Adam Jones into reality. Avoiding eye contact, he simply said, "Sorry."

It wasn't Adam's fault that the man's car was too far on his side of the road. Adam barely gave it a thought and maneuvered his way through the traffic. He had more important things to worry about. He was relieved to leave the Washington D.C. gridlock behind him.

His thoughts were elsewhere. He didn't remember turning onto an exit ramp north of the city. He was on a country road in Maryland now and felt as if he had the highway to himself. His long sandy hair flowed as he picked up speed.

A few minutes later, he pulled into a small town that left little to be desired. There were a few shops still open on the lackluster

Main Street. There was a small grocery store, a pharmacy, and a newsstand. A barber shop was on the corner. Most of the buildings had boarded up windows. Others were in desperate need of repair. He made a sharp right turn and eased up when he came to the only traffic light in town. He asked a motorist directions to Pine Meadow Hospital which was about three miles outside of town. He followed the curving path into the entrance lined with pine trees and slipped into a motorcycle spot. He walked hurriedly down a cobblestone walkway leading to the front door. He stepped to his right to avoid being sprayed by a sprinkler. There was a row of rose bushes nearby.

He pushed through a revolving door and walked hurriedly across the marble floor. It was an expansive lobby, with a ten foot tall fountain and hanging plants next to it. Visitors and patients with walkers sat in a lounge near the information desk. Medical staff milled alongside people in a hurry to look in on sick friends and relatives.

Adam went to the gift shop to look for flowers. He was just trying to put off going to see her. He was not good at these things and never knew what to say. He bought a dozen red roses and followed a sign for the elevator. He got off on the fifth floor and wound his way through endless winding corridors until he found the Intensive Care unit. He circled around the monitor desk that was dead center, and saw nurses in annoying to the eyes pink outfits, hovering over laptops. He checked numbers. All the rooms looked alike. He found his mother's room and stood in the door a moment before entering. She was a pathetic sight, lying in bed with tubes in her nose. Her face was pale and gaunt looking. Her eyes were bright red.

"Hello, Ma," he said brightly. "I came as fast as I could."

He laid the flowers on the bedside table and leaned over to kiss her on the cheek.

"You gotta stop this. You'll kill yourself if you keep it up."

"Would it make a difference?" Her voice was barely audible over the sounds of machines hooked up to her.

"I talked to the doctor and he said you had a bad fall. You had too much to drink is more like it."

She groaned and waved her hand. "I'll be fine."

"You aren't fine. Your face. Look at it--all bruised up like that. You look like you're on your last legs!"

She coughed and said, "It could only be too soon. But we know why I'm here, don't we?"

He rubbed her hand and sighed. "I know. We could have solved this whole thing if--"

"I don't want you to get involved in my disputes," she said with effort.

"I want this to be over with. It's gone on long enough. Ma, I want you in Rehab and I want you to stay there till you get help."

"You're feisty today." She coughed again.

"Don't you see what you've become? You're a bitter woman. It isn't right and I swear I'll do something about it."

"It's my fight."

There was a long, uncomfortable silence. He scrambled for something to talk about. He went over to the window and looked out. This time, her room overlooked the Emergency Room parking lot at the back of the hospital. Ambulance drivers waited in line to pull up to the revolving doors. He saw the back door of one of the vehicles open. Two paramedics scrambled out and pulled out an injured man on a stretcher. He watched them disappear from view around a large pillar, then glanced up and saw a helicopter pad on the roof. He looked on the window sill and grabbed a newspaper on the shelf. He pulled up a chair across from her and sat down.

He scanned the front page headlines and leafed through it. There were no stories of earthshattering importance, so he placed it on his lap.

"Do you remember the favor I asked you?" she asked.

"Yes, Ma."

She leaned forward and rasped, "Did you do as I asked?"

"No, but it will be taken care of."

"Oh, good." She sounded more at ease now.

"Don't worry, I'll take care of it. Rest easy."

Peter Molloy could not be controlled by his poor parents. When he turned fourteen, it was off to boarding school in the middle of a corn field in Nowhere, Pennsylvania. His father, Seth, reasoned that a change of scenery would do him a world of good. It would do more good for Seth's nerves if his surly son went away.

After two years of a rigorous academic grilling at Broad Meadow, Peter had calmed himself down. He was on the Honor Roll for the second year in a row. Despite his academic achievements, he still had a temper, and was not shy about speaking his mind. His loud mouth often got him in trouble. He was usually forgiven though, because he was so helpful and studious in the teacher's eyes.

One Thursday afternoon in April, Peter was studying in his dorm's lounge. Stewart Hall boys gathered around the TV, watching a lame talk show. He was concentrating more on who the possible daddies were to women on the panel, than he was on his Biology assignment. Video games blared in the background. By the end of the hour, his friends laughed and hollered when the paternity results were announced.

"No way!" they shouted.

Peter shook his head and grunted. "I knew it!"

"I thought it was the dude with all the tattoos!" Scott Baker blurted.

Greg could not have disagreed more. "Really? I thought for sure it was the guy with the nipple rings!"

Peter rolled his eyes and said, "Can't you guys watch something more interesting than this? These shows insult my intelligence."

"You don't have that far up to go, Molloy," chided Scott.

"I can't believe they're actually gonna let you graduate in a few weeks," Peter shot back.

"If we don't learn this stuff now, we won't be prepared for the real world," he reasoned.

"It's true," agreed Greg. "They don't teach this stuff here."

"It's high time they did," Scott said.

"Knock it off, you guys!" Peter growled.

Greg grunted and said, "Who pissed in your corn flakes?"

"Go to hell!" Peter looked back at his notes and stretched his feet on the coffee table.

The next show was more lame than the previous one. Now, everybody had to guess the guests correct gender. The boys erupted into fits of laughter when a dim-witted guy found out his girlfriend was really a man in drag!

Peter glared at the TV screen and shook his head in disgust. "You've gotta be kidding!"

Everyone laughed, except Peter. He reached in his pants pocket and pulled out his cell phone. He popped open the lid and checked messages. Nothing. He continued reading, but couldn't concentrate.

A few minutes later, he checked messages again. Still nothing. He navigated to his address list and punched his home phone number. When his mother answered, he gave her a litany of complaints.

"I need to talk to Dad. It's important."

"Can I help you?"

"No, I have to talk to him."

"He went fishing at the lake."

"Oh," he whined.

"He would've taken you guys, but he really needed time to himself. Maybe you can go with him next week."

"Yeah, right."

"Peter, I know when something's not right. You whine when you get upset. What's wrong, honey?"

"It's personal."

"It's something a mother can't talk to her son about. Is it about a girl?"

"Something like that."

"I'll give him the message. I'm sorry your Mother can't help you."

"Not with this. You understand."

"Yeah, I think I do." She giggled, remembering what it was like to be young and in love.

"It isn't funny. Good-bye!" He slammed the lid shut and stomped back to his room. He plopped on his bed and stared out the window.

About half an hour later, the door opened and Peter looked up to see the tall, burly frame of his roommate, Todd Curtis, enter the room. He removed his baseball cap and laid it on the desk. He peeled off his grass stained uniform and changed into his sweats.

"What's wrong?" Todd asked. "You look upset."

"I'll be okay."

Seth Molloy arrived home late Sunday night feeling revigorated after having spent a few days fishing at his cabin on a lake. You couldn't ask for better weather. A day in the sun yielded a bucket full of striped bass, along with a nasty sun burn. His forehead got the brunt of it. He arrived home exhausted late Sunday night. He went to his office at seven o'clock sharp Monday morning and caught up on paperwork.

Seth was the definition of success. He attended all the right schools. He played football at Temple University. He passed the bar exam on his second try. He spent long, grueling hours as a paralegal at a prestigious firm in Philadelphia. Later on, he developed a reputation as a Pit Bull defense attorney. He was a wizard at rendering jurors into a state of absolute confusion, thereby producing the desired result he wanted, insufficient proof of a client's guilt. Sometimes when he got his clients off on a technicality, he wondered if they were actually guilty. Prosecutors despised the man. Powerful defense attorneys in the Philadelphia area clamored to work with him. When the stress of city life took its toll on him, he moved to the Townsend area, and worked at an office on Chestnut Street. It was a small firm, and he shined as its star defense lawyer.

At some point he developed a conscience, if it could be called that, and became a prosecutor. Every so often, he crossed paths with Philadelphia prosecutors who secretly loathed him. Others didn't keep their feelings secret. Most of the time they tried to hold in their resentment when they worked on cases together.

Molloy had a lot of enemies. And not all of them were criminals he helped get one way tickets to prison.

No one would have guessed he was in his mid-fifties. He was in better shape than a lot of men younger than he was. He worked out twice a week, and tried to make time to play tennis. He had dyed jet black hair, and dressed for success in tailored suits.

He was poring over a legal brief when the telephone rang, interrupting his concentration. His receptionist was on the other line.

"What is it?" he snapped. "I'm busy."

"Raymond Sinclair is waiting to see you, sir."

"Tell him to make an appointment," Molloy growled back.

"He said it's urgent and that it can't wait."

Molloy glanced at his wristwatch. It was quarter to four. He groaned and said, "Send him in."

The door opened and he looked up to see the tall, slender figure of Raymond Sinclair enter the room. Clusters of dust lingered on the man's work clothes. Blue paint was splattered on his overalls.

Raymond grinned and shook Seth's hand. "Thanks for taking time to talk to me, Seth. I know you're busy, so I'll make it quick. I need your help."

Seth eyed him skeptically and grumbled. "What is it this time?"

"I'm in a bit of a bind. I know I promised I wouldn't ask you for any more money the last time. But it's an emergency."

"This again? It's always an emergency. I'm not a moneybag Ray! I told you last time I wouldn't help you out again. Twice is enough."

"I know it's a lot to ask."

Seth rolled his eyes. "That is an understatement."

"Debbie and I need help. She doesn't want you to know."

"I bet she doesn't. And this is supposed to help with your business?"

"Yes, we need some money for a project we're working on. I promise you, this will be the last time I come to you."

Seth cast a judgmental eye on him and said, "You bet it will be. Why should I help you? It seems funny that the money I lend you evaporates into thin air. What are you really spending it on? It certainly can't be for business expenses."

"Have compassion!" implored Sinclair.

"I've stopped caring what happens to you. This is the last time you come and scrounge off me. You hear me! I know about you. I hired a private investigator to check up on you. And he told me things I don't like. My money seems to not be going for what you claim you need it for. That could mean one of two things. Either you're using it for drugs or you're in debt with crooks. Debbie sure as hell isn't getting any of it–for your business."

"I can explain."

Seth looked sharply at the man. "I've heard all your excuses. Leave me alone!"

Raymond leaned forward and said, "You've got to help me."

"I'm a very patient man, Raymond, but you are wearing me down. Now get out."

"You'd better watch your back!"

"Is that a threat?"

"You can take it that way if you want," Raymond said on his way out.

Seth whistled and went back to work. About half an hour later, the telephone rang and he punched the speaker phone.

"This is Seth Molloy. How may I help you?"

There was static on the other end. Then he heard "Bye Bye Miss American Pie" in the background. It was the same song playing the last time the person called. The words had been changed to *Today'll be the day that you die. Today'll be the day that you die. Bye Bye Miss American Pie...*

"I don't know who you are, but I can find out!" Seth shouted. "Then I'll put you away for harassment!"

It played for a few more seconds, then the phone went dead. Seth hung up quickly. His palms were cold and clammy. He had trouble concentrating on the legal brief. He wanted to know who the sick bastard was who was making these crank calls?

He pulled open the desk drawer and read the note that had been left under the door when he returned from lunch that read: YOU'RE A DEAD MAN MOLLOY! Its letters had been cut out from magazines and pasted haphazardly on the page.

He stuck his Smith and Wesson .38 in his jacket pocket and went into the lobby. The room was empty. Everyone had gone home for the day. He exited the building and looked over his shoulders as he walked to his car. Before getting in, he checked to see if anyone was in it. He got in and locked the doors. Then he pulled out of the parking lot and sped down the street.

Seth sat at the traffic light on Main Street and was shocked to see the diner was boarded up. Nothing ever seemed to stay more than a year or so at that spot. He dismissed it as bad management. It was at a good location. Customers always filled benches, waiting to get in on Saturday nights.

A couple minute's later, he turned right onto Elm Street. He waved at neighbors out for a late afternoon stroll. It was the friendly atmosphere that drew him to the development when he moved to town more than twenty years ago. His house stood prominently in the middle of the street. There were white pillars on a brick front porch. The siding was eggshell blue. It had a big yard with a sprawling oak tree and rose bushes below the living room window. There was a basketball hoop on the driveway, that drew kids there like a magnate. It was a great place to raise a family.

Seth parked the car long enough to scoop up the newspaper on the lawn, then pulled into the two-car garage and entered through the family room door. He moved into the kitchen and reached for a wine glass on a rack hanging on the wall opposite the window. It was a nice sized room with a large island in the center. Marble counter tops offered plenty of space to prepare meals. The appliances fit in nicely with cherry red stained cabinets. Windows on a door to the back yard patio made the room look bright and cheerful. A beautiful view of the backyard swimming pool and trees could be seen out of the window over the sink. At this hour, rainbow patterns shot across the floor from a stain glass nature scene hanging in front of the window. Across the room, there was a rack with knife blades of varying sizes and thicknesses. Pots and pans hung next to them. The wall paper had a barn yard theme. Refrigerator artwork boasted the Molloy children's masterpieces. Snapshots of their sons Peter and Michael in their Little League uniforms were held in place with magnates. Next to them, there was one of eight-year-old Bonnie hamming it up for the camera in her ballet tutu.

To the left, a curved entryway led to the seldom used dining room. The walls were decorated with abstract oil paintings of beach scenes. Ladder-back chairs were set around a long table. Potted plants were set on a bay window. Another entryway led to the living room. It was eloquently decorated with antique furniture. Seth was usually so busy at work, that they seldom entertained.

Most of the action took place in the family room at the back of the house. A plush leather sofa and chairs were arranged in a semi circle around a glass coffee table. An oil painting of a forest scene hung over the sofa. The entertainment center was at the far end of the room. To the right, there was a stone fire place with family photos on the mantel. A large family portrait was in the middle. Games and puzzles were neatly stacked on a book shelf. A sliding door led out to the swimming pool deck.

The TV was blaring when Seth moved into the den. He set the wine glass on the end table next to his relining chair and shot his twelve-year-old son an evil glare. "Turn it down!"

Michael did as he was told. Seth settled into his seat and unfolded the newspaper.

A few minutes later, Molloy had just changed into more comfortable clothes, when he saw his wife, Debbie, heading down the hall in a bright blue evening dress. Her blonde hair was neatly pulled back with a beret. He met her at the top of the stairs and said, "You're going out with him, aren't you?"

"Do you always have to be jealous every time I meet with other men?"

He shook his index finger at her and shouted, "I know what you two are doing! He's no good for you."

"You're just jealous that another man has taken an interest in me," she said as she descended the steps.

Michael and Bonnie peered out of their bedroom doors and Debbie lowered her tone. "I want a word with you in private."

Seth's study advertised his importance. The walls were adorned with metals and accolades for his work in the community. His law degrees hung prominently in the center, with track lights shining on them. The shelves were lined with leather bound law books. His mahogany desk was massive, and made those who gathered around it feel insignificant. Framed family pictures stood in between piles of case files and folders.

They went into the room and Seth locked the door. He eyed her coldly.

"This has gone on long enough, Seth. I want a divorce."

Taken aback, he said, "I'm sorry you feel that way."

"I don't want to have a dragged out legal mess in court for visitation rights."

"I'm sure we can come up with a fair solution."

"It's better this way."

He looked at her incredulously and said, "Have you learned nothing from years being married to a lawyer?"

She eyed him suspiciously. "What are you talking about?"

"Do you really think the court will award custody to a tramp like you?"

"What are you talking about?"

"Don't try to pretend that you two aren't an item."

"We work together. I would never cheat on you."

"My private detective can prove otherwise. Or would you like to see the pictures?"

"What pictures?"

"The ones of you two in intimate situations."

"We would never–"

He went over to his desk and pulled open the top drawer. He reached for a manilla envelope and dumped the contents on the blotter. She looked in horror at images of her and Raymond in bed together.

"We didn't sleep with each other," she said.

"The pictures prove otherwise."

"I'll just get an expert to prove they're fake."

"Go ahead, but a judge might not agree. I have a lot of friends in the courthouse."

She gave him the evil eye. "You wouldn't dare."

"Try me. I'll see to it that you don't get custody of the kids."

"You bastard!"

"Don't think I won't do it."

She picked up the framed portrait of them on their wedding day that was on his desk, and flung it across the room. The glass smashed into a million pieces. Then she spun on her heels and was on her way out, when he grabbed her left arm. "Raymond is no good for you, Debbie. He'll only bring you down!"

"You're hurting me! Let me go!" She pulled free, and the sleeve ripped on her outfit. "Now look what you've done!"

She ran out and Seth kept up the pace. "Raymond's robbing you blind and you don't know it!"

"Leave me alone!" her voice shook.

The children were now standing at the top of the steps, listening to their parent's arguing again, as usual. They heard him scream, then saw her burst out of the room. Then they saw him go after her.

"Leave me alone!" Debbie shouted back at him. She slipped into the powder room, opened her purse and pulled out a safety pin. She lifted her ripped sleeve and somehow managed to get it back together again. She looked at her tired, worn out reflection and wondered how she had gotten to look so old. Years ago, she got into arguments with her family when the subject of Seth Molloy came up. They warned her not to marry him but she was so blinded by love, she refused to listen to them. Now she was paying the price for her stubbornness.

She wiped away tears, and dabbed her face with a Kleenex. She reapplied blush on her cheeks and headed out. She went to the foot of the steps and shouted, "Come along, Bonnie!"

Bonnie leaned on her crutches and teetered one step at a time as she descended the stairs. Her cast made a thumping sound every time it hit the wall. When she reached the marble floor, she hobbled over to kiss her father good-bye. She slowly approached the door and went outside. Debbie glared back at her husband and slammed the front door on her way out. Bonnie eased her way down the porch steps and across the driveway. Then Debbie helped her into the car.

Michael and Seth heard the car engine start. Then they heard the tires screech out of the driveway and down the street. Seth looked up at Michael and said, "What are you staring at? Go to your room!"

Debbie took time out to stop at the deli on Main Street and got a sub for Bonnie. Ten minutes later, she drove down Main Street and parked behind the Learning Center. She helped Bonnie out of the car and into the building. She popped her head in the classroom and saw the teacher setting up for the seven o'clock session. It was a large room with tables of various sizes and heights jammed next to each other. A combination of glue and paints of various colors were slapped on the tops. Mismatched chairs were lined up across from the work areas.

She told the teacher that she was late getting to a business function and asked if Bonnie could eat her dinner at her desk. The teacher told her it was all right, and Debbie kissed her daughter on the forehead.

"When you're finished eating, draw me a masterpiece that I can add to your refrigerator artwork."

Bonnie grinned and said, "Okay, Mommy."

Debbie smiled back and walked hurriedly out of the room. She glanced at her wristwatch and went out to the parking lot.

A large sign with the Chamber of Commerce logo hung on a restaurant wall. Men and women drummed up business over cocktails and hors d'oeuvres. Raymond Sinclair sat at the bar drinking a martini, watching them mingle. He was irritated that Debbie forced this on him. He detested events like this. He was not good at the art of small talk. He had nothing in common with these people. It bored him to tears having to listen to their endless spiels about their businesses. He could care less and hoped his lack of interest didn't show through when he talked to them. He finished his drink and laid it on the bar. It was about quarter after six.

He pushed his way through the crowd and waited by the entrance. Debbie collected her portfolio case and walked hurriedly into the restaurant. Raymond patted her shoulder and sized her up. Her face was flushed and she was out of breath.

He leaned in and she turned her head for a kiss on the cheek. "Hi Debbie."

She feigned a cheerful grin and said, "Hi. Sorry I'm late."

He put his arm around her waist as they headed toward the private dining room. "You look upset. What's wrong?"

"I just told Seth I want a divorce."

He lowered his voice. "Are you sure that's what you want to do?"

"I've thought it over carefully. It's the only way."

"If that's what you want, then I'm okay with it. How did he take it?"

"Not well. We got into an argument."

"What else is new?"

"I can't stand the way things are going."

He reached out to touch her hand and she put her hand on his. "What are we going to do?"

"I don't know," he said glumly.

They put on name tags for their business, Dazzling Interiors, and blended with the crowd. A waitress walked by and Debbie took a glass of wine. Raymond stood by her side smiling occasionally as she talked about their business. He glanced at the clock over the bar and grimaced. It was going to be a long evening.

Peter's mind was on other things. He stared at his History text and could not comprehend an entire passage he had just read. He referred to his notes, but that wasn't much good either. Todd leaned his back against the wall and flipped a page from his spiral notebook. He glanced over at his roommate and said, "What's wrong? You're making me nervous."

"I got into a fight with my mom when she called me this afternoon."

"What was it this time? Talk to me."

Peter turned to face him and said, "Not now. It's hard to talk about."

"Well, I'm always here you know. We can talk about it when you've calmed down."

Peter closed his book and got to his feet. He grabbed his skateboard and leather jacket and headed out.

"I'll be back in a few minutes."

Todd smiled and said, "See you."

Peter walked hurriedly out of the room. About five minutes later, Todd heard a motorcycle speed out of the parking lot.

Peter sped down the country roads on his Harley. The wind whipping into his face brought tears to his eyes. He was so upset at the moment, he could have been shedding real ones. He pulled into a park about five miles from campus and slowed to a stop. He untied the skateboard, and glided over to the ramps. A few younger kids skated nearby. They flew off the ramp and landed smoothly on the pavement. It was not long before he was airborne too. When it started to get dark, he hopped back on his motorcycle and sped back onto the country road.

Edna and John Wilcox gazed at before and after photographs in Debbie's portfolio. The rooms took on a new life. They were brighter and appeared larger than life.

About quarter after seven, Debbie glanced at her wristwatch and said, "I'm sorry to cut our little talk short, but I need to go to the office before I have to pick up my daughter from her art class at the Creative Learning Center."

She rose and they exchanged pleasantries. "It was nice to meet with you."

"Likewise," they said in unison.

About fifteen minutes later, Raymond led the group out.

"You two make a great team," John said.

"Thank you, Mr. Wilcox. I hope you will consider us."

Edna grinned and said, "We'll let you know."

He thanked them and headed to his car. The confrontation with Seth a few hours earlier was all he could think about. Sometimes he didn't think life was fair. How did Debbie end up with such an awful man? For her sake, Raymond hoped that she would leave the man.

He witnessed first hand the pain that she was going through. She told him things that Seth had done. He wished he could eliminate Seth. He had a key to the house. He knew his patterns. It would be easy...

Five minutes later, he reached the fork in the road. Instead of turning left to go to his apartment, he went the other way. He crossed Main Street, headed toward Debbie's house.

Seth couldn't get that song out of his head. He whistled *Bye Bye Miss American Pie* while he showered. About seven thirty, he grabbed a towel, climbed out of the bathtub and dried off before going to his bedroom. His whistling grew louder as he put on his bathrobe. He started to go out, when a flash of paranoia overcame him. He reached in his underwear drawer and grabbed his gun. He put it in his pocket and headed down the hall.

Michael's room was eerily quiet as he went past it. He usually had to pound on the door to get his attention over the ear-shattering music that blasted out of the boy's boom box.

He knocked and stuck his head in the door. "Michael?" he asked with uncertainty. The boy wasn't there. Seth flicked on the light switch at the top of the steps and proceeded downstairs.

Carolyn van Horn glanced at her wristwatch. It was about eight o'clock. She waited for Roxy, her four-year-old Golden Retriever to sniff a blade of grass. The sound of a car backfiring startled both of them. Roxy pricked up her ears and bounded down the sidewalk. The elastic leash snapped taught and slipped from Carolyn's right hand. It took almost all her strength to hold it in both hands, as the terrified dog bounded down the sidewalk.

"Whoah, whoah, Roxy!" she screamed in alarm.

Carolyn pulled back as hard as she could, and yanked at the dog's collar so hard, that Roxy stopped in her tracks. She leaned down and rubbed Roxy's neck.

"I'm sorry, girl," she said in a childlike tone. "You had a scare."

She looked up in time to see a bearded man fleeing from the Molloy's house. He clutched his right shoulder, scrambled into a tan van on the curb, and sped away.

Carolyn reluctantly crossed the street and looked down. Roxy relentlessly sniffed the macadam. Carolyn reached in her jacket pocket with her free hand and pulled out a small flashlight. She pointed it toward the ground and saw blood spots.

"Oh no," she murmured.

☆   ☆   ☆

Michael wiped a bead of perspiration off his forehead. His thoughts were elsewhere. Jeff was creaming him. A green monster clobbered him and there was a loud explosion.

Jeff stared blankly at him and said, "What's wrong with you man?"

"Nothing." He smashed Jeff's green man into smithereens and pressed the joy stick so hard it was a wonder it didn't break.

"Ease up! What's your problem?"

Michael glanced at the clock again and said, "I'm okay."

They continued zapping monsters and Michael didn't give it another thought.

Debbie and Bonnie returned home about nine o'clock.

"We're back!" Debbie shouted. She went into the family room, turned on the lights and saw chairs knocked over. Bonnie was right behind her.

"Honey go to your room," Debbie commanded.

"What's wrong?" she squawked.

"Just do as I say!" She kissed her curly blonde locks and said, "I'll read you a story in a few minutes."

Bonnie's eyes brightened. "I can't wait!"

Debbie frowned as she watched Bonnie slowly make her ascent upstairs. Then she cautiously went into the living room to investigate. A window was broken. A table was overturned. A poker was lying by the couch. She went over to the fireplace and reluctantly looked down. She screamed, when she saw Seth lying at her feet.

She checked his pulse and gasped, "Oh my God! He's dead!"

☆   ☆   ☆

CHAPTER 2

Detective Frank Logan had survived his first year in the rural community of Townsend. After high school, he graduated from the Police Academy, and worked at the same Philadelphia precinct as his father, Francis. Sadly, they never got a chance to work alongside each other. When Frank was in junior high school, Francis was gunned down. The memory haunted Frank to this day. He always worked hard, hoping that Francis would approve. Frank made detective before his thirtieth birthday, but the stress of city life got too much for him. He transferred to Townsend and struggled to fit into the slower lifestyle. It was a small staff, and detectives often had to do the jobs that criminalists did in the city.

When he first arrived in Townsend, he was often mistaken for a kid barely out of high school. It was his youthful appearance that annoyed him to no avail. He tried to work out on a regular basis and had the rock-hard physique to prove it. Now he sported a mustache to make himself look older.

Everybody at the police station knew Seth Molloy. They were all in shock when they got the call. He had a reputation as a tough prosecutor. He could render witnesses into piles of mush. Or he could smooth talk them into saying the wrong thing. In the short time that Logan had been in Townsend, he had the misfortune to be interrogated by Molloy on the witness stand. Colleagues were right when they warned him to think carefully before answering his questions.

Logan arrived at the scene about ten p.m. and made a mental note of the family room. The victim was lying on his back near the fireplace. A metal poker was beside him. Blood streaked from the top of his head down his face. Blood spots soaked his white robe. There was also a purple stain on it. The collar was ripped. It was opened enough at the top to reveal a scratch on his chest. A Smith and Wesson was lying on the floor about five feet away. Chairs were strewn about. An end table was lying on its side and a lamp was about a foot away from it. A broken wine glass lay nearby. One poker was lying near the sofa. Shattered glass nicknacks had fallen off a shelf and were scattered near the body. At the center of the stone fireplace mantel, a framed portrait of the smiling, happy family stood as a haunting reminder of what could have been. On either side there were framed family snapshots in happier times.

A photographer took pictures of the grisly scene. Criminalist Jim Anderson put the gun in an evidence bag. Then he placed index cards along each of Molloy's fingernails and put evidence bags on his hands up to the wrists.

"What's going on?" Logan asked Officer Brody McGlaughlin.

"It's just your average burglary/homicide. It looks like the victim was in the wrong place at the wrong time and the burglar killed him."

He led Logan into the kitchen and pointed to various household appliances on the floor by the back door. Logan jotted a list that included a flat-screen TV, a DVR, a radio, a laptop, and a microwave oven. The window on the kitchen door had a hole on the pane closest to the doorknob. Broken glass was on the floor in front of the door. A bullet casing was found under the table. There was a bullet hole in the kitchen window. Logan leaned on the counter and examined it. He glanced down and followed blood splotches to the back door.

He went outside and turned on his flashlight. He pointed the beam toward the broken window and saw shards of glass on the ground. He followed the blood stains to the side of the house. The trail led past the basketball hoop in front of the garage, and onto the driveway. They ended at the curb in front of the house. Officers were photographing the spots and placing evidence cards at each blood stain site.

Logan went back into the kitchen and wrote "bullet hole in kitchen window" in his pad. Then he reached in his jacket pocket and pulled out a tape measure. He went over to the door and jotted down the dimensions of the hole above the doorknob. Then he went through an entryway leading to the family room and saw Coroner Stan Green hovering over the body, taking notes. Logan knelt next to him and asked, "Do you have any idea what time Molloy died?"

"I'll know more when I examine the body," Stan said without looking up from the corpse.

Logan went back into the kitchen and glanced at peaceful water color landscapes that adorned the foyer walls as he went by. He went out the front door and looked down at the porch and steps. Nothing seemed out of the ordinary. He saw a forty-something blonde woman standing behind the police barricade tape, her arms wrapped tightly around a gangly looking boy in nylon sweats and a little girl with a cast on her leg. Neighbors lined up on the sidewalk, watching officer's every movements, with avid curiosity. Others peered out at the flashing police patrol lights from their front doors, wondering what was happening. Others watched at a safe distance across the street. They were talking and whispering to each other. An older woman went up to the horrified family and wrapped her arms around them at the same time.

"Oh, Debbie," she said. "Please let me know if there is anything I can do to help."

Debbie's voice trembled. "Thanks, Helen."

"Who would do such a thing? It's just horrible."

Logan went up to them and introduced himself. He noticed the younger woman's face looked puffy and red from crying.

"I'm sorry about your husband," he said. "I know you've had a real shock, but I need to ask some questions."

Helen reached for the children's hands and quietly excused herself. They went over to the group huddled on the driveway, and waited patiently for Debbie to join them.

Debbie wiped tears from her eyes.

"What time did you find the body, Mrs. Molloy?"

"About nine o'clock. I just came back from picking up my daughter from the Creative Learning Center on Main Street."

"Was anyone in the house at the time?"

She shook her head and pointed to Michael, who was standing with the others, looking at his shoes. "My son was at a friend's house down the street."

They went over to Michael and Logan said, "Your mother told me you were at a friend's house."

"Yeah, we were playing video games till she called and told me somebody broke into the house."

"You didn't see or hear anything suspicious?"

"No."

Logan looked at the cast on Bonnie's right leg.

"She had a ballet injury a few weeks ago," Debbie explained.

"That's too bad," Logan said. "It must've hurt."

Bonnie crinkled her nose and said, "That's for sure."

Logan looked back at Debbie and asked, "Do you have any other children, Mrs. Molloy?"

"My son, Peter. He's sixteen. He's a sophomore at Broad Meadow."

"That's a really tough school," Logan commented.

"He's a hard worker." She closed her eyes and put her hand on the bridge of her nose. "I have to call him and let him know." She burst into tears. "They were so close."

"Do you want an officer to talk to him?"

She ran her hand through her hair and said, "No, I don't want him to find out that way. I have to do this. Can I go back in and get my cell phone?"

"I'm afraid not, ma'am," he told her. "Not until we're finished investigating. I'm sorry."

"That's okay."

Logan watched her go over to a man standing on the sidewalk. A moment later, he reached in his pant's pocket and handed her a cell phone. She found a quiet spot by her mini van and pulled open the lid. She seemed to have difficulty handling someone else's phone. Without the address list handy, it looked like she was having trouble remembering the number. At that moment, a tall, slender middle-aged man went up and pecked her on the cheek. He gave her a hug and the safety pin on her sleeve came undone and she fastened it again with her right hand. She didn't think anyone noticed, but Logan did.

"Oh, Raymond," her voice trembled. "Thank God you're here!"

He took the phone out of her hand and said, "Here, let me call him. It isn't something you should have to do." He dialed Peter's number.

"Hello?" grumbled Peter.

"Hi Peter. It's Raymond."

"Oh, hi. It's kind of late. I was just getting ready for bed."

"Peter, I have to tell you something."

"What's wrong?"

"I don't know how to tell you this." He fell silent.

"What's wrong?"

"Oh Peter, it's horrible. When your mother came back from picking up Bonnie from her art class tonight, she found your father on the floor. Somebody broke into the house and--and–"

"Oh my God! Is he okay?"

"It's the worst thing in the world! Somebody hit him on the head. He didn't make it."

"I'll be there right away!"

Raymond hung up and handed the phone back to Debbie's neighbor. He rubbed her shoulder. She was more distraught than before. Michael put his arm around her to help calm her down. Logan went back over to them and Raymond introduced himself. "I'm Raymond Sinclair, a friend of the family. Did anybody see who did this?"

"We're talking to neighbors now," Logan answered. "What was your relationship to the deceased?"

"I'm a business associate of Debbie's."

"We operate an interior design company," Debbie explained. "He's my partner."

"Where were you tonight?" he asked Sinclair.

"Debbie and I were at a business function at the Garden Terrace restaurant. We were talking to potential clients."

Logan looked back at Debbie and said, "I know it's hard talking about these things now, but it has to be done. Did your husband have enemies, ma'am?"

"I don't know." Her voice wavered. "He had...clients...a lot of them...and, as a prosecutor he put a lot of people in jail."

"That means any ex-con with a grudge could have done this."

"Everybody liked him," Raymond said. "He was a pillar of the community. I can't imagine anyone wanting to hurt him."

"You would be surprised what people are capable of," Logan said flatly.

"Seth must have caught the thief by surprise," Sinclair suggested.

"That's what we think," Logan agreed.

Raymond looked at Debbie and asked, "Is there anything missing?"

"Not that I know of. But I'm sure I'll know soon enough."

"How did you rip your sleeve, Mrs. Molloy?" Logan asked.

She bowed her head and said, "I was in such a hurry to get to the restaurant that it ripped when I was going out the door. I had to take time to find a safety pin."

Logan asked some more questions and Sinclair interrupted, bitterly. "Please Detective, can't you see that she's had enough?"

"I understand that sir, but we have formalities. But, I think I've gotten enough information for now. I'll have to talk to you later when you have time to get used to it."

"People never get used to such a thing," Sinclair boomed.

She gripped his hand and said, "He's only doing his job, Raymond." She looked back at the kids and said, "Michael, why don't you take Debbie back to Jeff's house?"

"It's kind of late, isn't it?"

Debbie rubbed her face and thought carefully for a moment. Helen patted her shoulder and said, "I'll take them with me. Come on kids, the detective needs to ask her some more questions."

"But I should be here," Michael protested.

Helen patted his shoulder and said, "You can be with her later."

"Thanks, Helen," Debbie said.

The older woman held their hands and walked down the street. When they were gone, Logan said, "We need to search the rest of your house, if you don't mind."

"Go ahead," she said.

He offered them his condolences and left them alone. He went upstairs and looked around in the master bedroom. He saw a wallet on the bureau and opened it. It contained a wad of bills inside. Maybe the burglar did not have time to go upstairs. He checked the contents and saw a business card for a private detective named Luke Springer. Nothing else seemed out of place. His clothes were neatly stacked in the drawers. Suit jackets hung in the closet. Mrs. Molloy's outfits were the only thing missing. It didn't look like they slept together in the same room. He went across the hall and stuck his head in the door. High-heeled shoes were under a chair. A brush and makeup kit were on the bedside table.

Logan went into Molloy's study that was next door. He went over to the trash can by the door and sifted through papers and other throw away items. At the bottom of the basket, there was a broken picture frame with shattered glass. He pushed his hands further down and retrieved part of a ripped portrait of Debbie and Seth. He started to go over to the desk, when he saw a long strip of paper on the rug. He leaned down to pick it up. It felt like photographic paper. It looked like part of an arm, but he couldn't tell. The shredder was by the desk. He leaned down and scooped up remaining strips still in the machine and put them in evidence bags. Then he checked files on the desk, and jotted down cases Seth was working on. The drawers contained office supplies and business cards. Old matchbooks were stuffed in the middle drawer. He glanced at the desk calendar and saw a note to meet with a body guard the next day. His telephone number was circled in red ink.

He sifted through a trash can by the desk and discovered a wadded up note that had letters cut out from magazines that read, "YOU'RE A DEAD MAN MOLLOY."

Detective Joe Flosky was a country boy who grew up on a farm near Townsend. He joined the Police Academy out of high school, and spent most of his early law enforcement career handing out parking tickets on Main Street. Townsend left little to be desired in the homicide department. Other than the regular weekend arrests of drunk and disorderly patrons at the local bar, country life offered peace and tranquility. As a rooky, he often got stuck with jobs his superiors did not want to do.

On the threshold of thirty, he dreamed of settling down if he ever crossed paths with the right woman. The drawback of living in such a small community was, that either women were taken or they were dating someone. But that never stopped Flosky from trying. Though he was not a matinee idol like some of his younger colleagues, he made up for it in intelligence. He was five foot four, with a dark crew cut and a ruddy complexion and a gap in his teeth. Social gatherings started whenever he entered the room. Friends often said he was the life of the party.

When he stepped up to Carolyn van Horn to ask her questions, Roxy lunged at him and launched into a barking fit. She yanked the dog's collar with all her might, and rubbed her back. Joe held out his hand to appease the growling Golden Retriever, but Roxy would have none of that. She practically took off one of his fingers. Joe cringed and backed away from the snarling canine. Carolyn rubbed Roxy's neck and apologized profusely.

"She was barking so loud I thought I was going to go deaf," she recalled.

"What time was that?"

"About eight o'clock. I always walk Roxy at the same time every night."

"Did you see or hear anything unusual before you took her for the walk?" he shouted to be heard over the barking.

Still pulling Roxy back, she raised her voice and said, "Not really. I spend most of the time in my family room. It's at the back of the house. We wouldn't even hear a bomb blow up, with the TV blaring. We were in the middle of watching a *Matlock* marathon."

"How long did you walk the dog?"

"About a half an hour."

"Did you see or hear anything unusual while you were walking her?"

"I thought I heard a car backfiring."

"When?"

"About eight o'clock."

"Are you sure?"

"I'm pretty sure. I think that was when Roxy started barking. Maybe she sensed something wasn't right before that. She was acting—well, peculiar. But she definitely knew something wasn't quite right. People can learn a lot from their pets."

"I bet they can," he agreed. "Did you see anybody leaving the Molloy's home?"

Roxy's barking grew more agitated. Carolyn leaned down to stroke her golden mane. "Come on Roxy, he's a nice man. I'm so sorry about this, Detective. She's a nervous Nellie tonight. But can you blame her, with all that's been going on? Police sirens flashing on and off. Cops going in and out of the house. People all over the place. The poor thing."

"I guess I'd be scared, if I were a dog," Flosky admitted. He repeated the question.

"I saw a man with long hair and a beard running out of the house. He was running kind of funny."

Flosky gave her a puzzled look. "What do you mean, ma'am?"

"Well, he was holding his arm and limping, or something. He got into a van in front of the house and sped off."

"What did it look like?"

"It was tan."

"Was there anything else noticeable about it?"

"It had a ladder on the top. It was one of those vans that doesn't have windows on the side."

"Do you remember anything else?"

She shook her head. "I hope I was of some help."

"You told me just what I wanted to hear. Thanks, ma'am."

He headed back toward the house and met Logan at the front door.

"Did you find out anything?" Frank asked.

Flosky waved his right hand and said, "Plenty!"

"Did neighbors see anything?"

"A lady thought she heard a car's engine backfiring about eight and her dog started barking."

"That could have been when the gun was fired. Anything else?"

"She saw a man run from Molloy's house and speed off in a tan van. What did you find out?"

"I found a crumpled up death threat in a trash can in Molloy's study."

Flosky whistled. "You don't say!"

At that moment, Lieutenant Harry Winters went up to them. He was a giant of a man, with a shaved head and a prominent mustache. His eyes were cold and harsh, and there was a scar above his right eyebrow.

"Did you find out anything new?" Logan asked him.

"It looks like a failed burglary attempt. Molloy was in the wrong place at the wrong time."

"That's what it looks like," Logan agreed. "Molloy must've caught the perp in the act and shot him. He must've dropped the loot as he was exiting the premises."

"And then he must've caught his accomplice in the act and there was a struggle," Winters added. "The person hit him on the head with the poker and must have gone out the back door. Did you check the other rooms?"

"Yeah, nothing looks out of place," Logan replied. "I guess the perps didn't have time to get upstairs." Then he told him about the death threat that he discovered. "There is a lot more to this than what we saw. Somebody was threatening him."

"So what do you think?" Lieutenant Winters asked.

"He was being threatened," Logan said. "If he had some enemies, he probably had that gun with him at all times. People can get paranoid if they think someone's after them. That person could have hit him on the head and made it look like there had been a struggle."

"Who would have been threatening him?" Harry wondered.

"That's what I'm going to find out."

☆　☆　☆

CHAPTER 3

Peter saw police car lights flashing from a block away. When he approached the house, he saw neighbors lined up on both sides of the street, watching the chaos that was unfolding in front of their eyes. He slowed to a stop and hopped off his Harley. He arrived in time to watch as his father's body was carried out of the house on a gurney. He went over to his mother and Raymond Sinclair who watched in horror from the sidewalk. They hugged each other, their bodies rocking to and fro. She was sobbing uncontrollably. Peter patted her back and spoke softly.

"Oh, Peter," she wailed.

"It's like a nightmare," Peter said. "Do they–do they know who did it?"

"Not yet."

"I'm sorry I wasn't here earlier."

"Don't worry," Raymond said. "You're here now."

They huddled as they watched the ambulance disappear from view down the street. By now, most of the neighbors had gone to bed. The few that remained kept at a safe distance, not knowing what to say. The remaining police officers and detectives talked amongst each other.

Detective Logan looked across at the boy with Debbie Molloy. He had on a gray hoodie and sweat pants and kept looking at the ground. He was so busy attending to details pertaining to the crime scene before calling it a night, that he did not have time to introduce himself. The poor boy looked sullen. It was understandable. He just lost his father at an early age. Logan knew the feeling. He looked back at his colleagues and continued canvassing the crime scene.

Townsend law offices were all conveniently located within walking distance of the courthouse. It was an old two story house probably built in the 1920s or 1930s that was converted into an office. It was painted Williamsburg blue with white trim. A large wooden sign swung on a post in front of the building. It had large black letters that read: "Lowel, Molloy, & Patterson, Attorneys At Law."

Logan felt an overwhelming feeling of gloom when he arrived there about nine a.m. Tuesday. Most of Seth's coworkers canceled their appointments and took the day off. Others kept busy so they didn't have to think about the tragedy.

Molloy's office overlooked Chestnut Street, which was three blocks from the courthouse. The floor boards were old and creaked beneath his weight as he walked across the room. Overstuffed burgundy leather chairs were gathered in a semicircle around his desk. A long conference table was across the room. Shelves were filled up with Criminal Justice books. They were thick, leather-bound editions. Case files were in neat piles on his desk. It looked like his schedule for April was a full one. To date, Molloy had a lot of meetings with lawyers and witnesses. His log was filled up until the end of the month, but he would not be able to make those appointments.

His desk drawers were neat and orderly like in his study. File cabinet drawers were locked so he went to ask receptionist Wendy Sweetman for a key. She was a plump woman in her mid-forties, smartly dressed in a gray jacket and dress, her flaming red hair tied neatly with a beret. Reading glasses were draped on a chain around her neck. Her face was puffy from crying so much, and her eyes were bloodshot.

She opened a safe under the desk and rummaged through a collection of keys. A couple minutes later, she handed Logan the one to Molloy's safe. He continued checking recent cases Seth was working on. Then, a large manilla envelope wedged in between two folders caught his attention. He removed it and poured out the contents on the desk. He leafed through rather intimate photos of Debbie and Raymond.

"It looks like they are more than just business partners," he muttered. He put a photo in his jacket pocket and put the rest back in the manilla envelope and shoved it back in the file cabinet. He went back to the waiting room and pulled a chair next to Wendy.

"What can you tell me about Mr. Molloy? I know it's hard. Take your time."

Wendy wiped away tears and said, "He was kind and compassionate. Who would have wanted to kill him?"

"That's what I am trying to find out."

"He was always looking out for people. I don't know how I can help you, but I'll try. I want you to catch the person that did this horrible thing! He was the hardest working prosecutor in this office. He had a lot of clients. And he rarely lost a case. That's because he was so devoted to his job and spent time after hours slaving over legal books. He would always go that extra mile."

"Ms. Sweetman, I imagine he must have made a lot of enemies as a prosecutor."

"He helped put a lot of criminals behind bars over the years. Maybe one of them got out and had a grudge."

"That's what I was thinking. At first, I thought it was just a botched burglary attempt."

"What made you think otherwise?"

"I found a note in his trash can." He reached in his jacket pocket and pulled out a copy of the death threat. He showed it to her and she cringed. "Do you know anybody that could have done this?"

She wiped away tears and said, "I'm sorry, I can't think of anyone off hand."

"Did you see or hear anything recently that might have seemed suspicious?"

She leaned forward and spoke in a hushed tone. "Now that you mention it, I did hear Mr. Molloy arguing with someone."

"Who was it?"

"It was his wife's business partner, Raymond Sinclair."

"What were they fighting about?"

"I couldn't make it out. It's not my place to eavesdrop. But you can hear things. I try not to listen. It's not my business. It was something about money."

"Was Mr. Molloy having financial difficulty?"

She shook her head. "I think Mr. Sinclair came to him to borrow money for their business."

"Is Mr. Sinclair's business in financial trouble?"

She shrugged her shoulders. "I wouldn't know. You'd have to ask him yourself. Mr. Molloy was extremely angry. It's not the first time Mr. Sinclair has been in to see him."

Logan raised an eyebrow and grunted. "You don't say. Did Mr. Sinclair ask to borrow money from Seth Molloy before?"

"A couple of times."

"Did they ever fight about it before?"

"No, I think Mr. Molloy got fed up with him this time. He said he wasn't going to lend him any more money."

"What did Mr. Sinclair do when he said that?"

"He got so angry, that he stormed out of the office and slammed the door! I have to admit, I was a bit shaken up."

"You don't say." Logan jotted it in his pad and closed the notebook. He got to his feet and started for the door. He turned and smiled at her. "Thank you, ma'am."

"I hope I was of some help, sir."

He smiled and said, "I think you were."

"I'll give you a call if I remember anything else."

Logan waited for Tanya Hawkes to get off the telephone. She was a striking figure with shoulder length auburn hair and high cheek bones. She had on a dark suit jacket and matching slacks. Paperwork lay in neat piles on her desk. Abstract oil paintings adorned the walls. Hanging potted plants were near the front window. Every so often, she smiled to let him know that she had not forgotten him, and politely found a way to finish her conversation. She hung up and said, "Good morning, Detective Logan. How can I help you?"

"I know it's hard, but I thought you might be able to give me some information about Seth Molloy."

"I don't know if I can be of any help."

"Sometimes what people think is unimportant can be very valuable information, Ms. Hawkes. How long did you work for Mr. Molloy?"

"About five years."

"I imagine he made some enemies over the years. Did he ever mention that he got death threats?"

"He put a lot of people in prison. He probably got a lot of threats. He just got used to it."

"Do you think somebody might have killed him intentionally?"

"Well, I don't think it was a burglary."

"Neither do I. That's why I thought you might be of some help. You worked closely with him. You must have seen or heard some things."

"I think there's more to this case than meets the eye. He had a lot of skeletons in his closet and kept quiet about things, if you know what I mean."

He reached in his jacket pocket and pulled out a Baggy that had a copy of the death threat in it. He handed it to her and said, "What do you make of it?"

A look of fear flashed in her eyes. She handed it back to him and said, "It's probably just a crank."

"Had he received notes like this before?"

"Yes, but he tried not to take them seriously."

"Do you know who might have sent it?"

She shrugged her shoulders and said, "I don't know. I could run psychological profiles for you. Maybe I could check records on released prisoners who might have sent it."

"You're efficient," Logan observed.

"I was a paralegal at his firm. Law students fought tooth and nail to be Seth Molloy's legal assistant."

"If you remember anything give me a call."

He thanked her and headed out. She looked out the window and watched him pull onto the street.

Logan ordered take out at a grill joint on Main Street and ate a burger and fries at his desk. He got on line and surfed the Internet while he ate. He did a Google search on SETH MOLLOY and the screen filled up with one article after another about the man's illustrious career in Philadelphia and Townsend. He clicked on Archives and compiled a list of ex-cons who might have had reason to want to pay him back the first chance they got when they were sprung.

The coroner's report arrived at the station about eleven thirty a.m. Wednesday. Seth Molloy died about eight p.m. Cause of death was from the hit on the forehead with the poker. The victim's fingerprints were found on one of the pokers. There were no prints on the one that was used to hit him on the head. Powder burn tests on the gun that was found on the floor indicated that Molloy did not fire the weapon, but his fingerprints were on it. The lab results of the victim's fingernail scrapings had not come in yet, so they would not know if he scratched his assailant during the struggle. It would take time for all of the other evidence uncovered at the crime scene to be analyzed. Logan finished reading the report and handed it to Joe Flosky.

"It looks like I was right," Logan said. "The killer made it look like a botched burglary attempt. There were no powder burns on Molloy's hand. But his prints were on it."

"Maybe he heard a noise downstairs and grabbed his gun," Flosky suggested. "He saw the loot on the floor and was about to shoot, when the perp surprised him and they struggled."

"That makes sense. The gun must've flown out of Molloy's hand during the struggle. And then he got conked on the head and fell down. Maybe the burglar panicked and fired a few shots at the window. His partner must've gotten shot in the shoulder as he was exiting the premises. And then he sped off in the van and left his partner to fend for himself."

"The lady could've been wrong. Maybe she was so distracted with her dog that she didn't see the other guy getting in the van."

"Or maybe they met up with each other later. Either way, we need to track them down."

Lieutenant Winters went over to them and read the report. When he was finished looking at it, he handed it to Logan and asked, "Any luck finding out who sent the death threats?"

Logan shook his head and grunted.

"Who would have been threatening him?" Flosky wondered.

"That's what I would like to find out," Logan said.

*   *   *

CHAPTER 4

About three o'clock, Logan went to Debbie Potter-Molloy's home and rang the doorbell.

Michael appeared at the door in his nylon sweats and said, "Oh, hello, Detective Logan."

"Hi Michael. I need to ask some more questions."

Michael led him into the den. Bonnie was playing with a doll by the TV. Debbie sat on a rocking chair gazing out the bay window. Logan saw a blond teenage boy on the couch doing homework and figured it must be Peter. They were quiet and the only sound he heard was from an episode of "Scooby Doo," that blared on an old-fashioned square TV. A lot of excess space was in the cabinet where the flat screen TV used to be.

Debbie got up and went over to him. "Good afternoon, Detective Logan. This is my oldest son, Peter." She pointed and smiled.

Logan reached out to shake his hand. "It's nice to meet you, Peter. I was so busy last night, that I didn't get a chance to talk to you when you got here. I'm so sorry for your loss."

"Thanks," Peter mumbled. He leaned back in his seat and looked at the TV.

Raymond Sinclair came in and handed Debbie a coffee mug. He waved to Logan and sat next to Peter.

"I know it's hard dealing with this, but it must be done," Logan said. "I have to ask some more questions."

"Michael, take Bonnie upstairs please," Debbie instructed.

"But, Mom," he whined.

"Do as I say."

Michael helped his little sister to her feet, and she hobbled behind him leaning on the crutches as she went up the steps leading into the kitchen. Peter went outside to talk to a friend on his cell phone.

Debbie turned to face the detective and said, "All right, how may I help you?"

"I have reason to believe there was more to this crime than a burglary. Someone wanted your husband dead."

Her eyes widened in alarm. "How do you know that?"

"Someone was sending him death threats. But I can't say anything else until I get more information. I'm going on a gut feeling."

A look of anguish shot across her face. "Oh, I see."

"I'm new to this area and had to do some research on your husband. It looks like he got a lot of clients off on technicalities when he was a defense attorney. Do you suppose somebody could have been holding a grudge all these years?"

"I don't know," she said. "Seth kept his cases confidential."

"Did Seth ever get death threats after he got his defendants off?"

Sinclair shook his head and said, "I don't know. If he did, he kept them secret. He had a gun...but he was probably playing it safe."

"As a prosecutor, he put a lot of people in prison. Did anybody ever get out and try to get back at him?"

"Somebody threw a rock in the window once," she said. "And we got a lot of crank calls."

"Anything else?"

She took a sip of coffee. "That was pretty much the extent of it. But Seth was a private man. If there were other...incidents...he would have kept them from me."

"Seth was immensely private, that's for sure," Raymond agreed.

"On the night of Seth's murder, I found a note that he wrote on his desk calendar," Logan said. "Did you know that he was going to meet with a body guard the next day?"

"When you deal with so many angry people, it is a wise thing to do, wouldn't you agree, Detective?" Raymond said.

Logan nodded his agreement.

"When did Seth decide to be a prosecutor?"

"About ten years ago," she said. "He got fed up defending clients he knew were guilty. He liked putting dirt bags away. But I had my reservations. I was carrying Bonnie, and well, I guess any expectant mother would have a few worries...like maybe someone would get off and come looking for him. He helped put a lot of criminals behind bars."

"Is that why he got the gun?"

"I guess so."

"He must have had a lot of threats over the years, if he put so many people away," Logan agreed. "Why else would he have gotten a gun?"

"He never talked about things like that. He didn't want to worry us."

"Are you sure? Think carefully. Is there anything at all that might stand out in your mind?"

He kept his eagle-like gaze on Debbie. She averted eye contact and said, "I can't think of anything."

"He hired a body guard after a high profile murder case," Sinclair volunteered.

"How did you know?"she asked.

"He told me. He didn't want me to tell you. He didn't want it to upset you."

She threw her hands in the air in frustration. "I can't believe he didn't tell me."

"Did he talk to you about anything else?" Logan asked him.

"No."

Logan looked back at Debbie and said, "Can I talk to your kids?"

"Go ahead." Debbie showed him to Bonnie's room and listened outside the door.

He went inside and saw her sitting on the floor playing with a Barbie doll. He looked across the room at stuffed animals lined up in a row on a shelf. Next to it, a pile of dolls lay on her bed as if they were waiting for her to play with them. He used his best childlike tone. "Hi Bonnie. Can I talk to you?"

"Okay."

"How do you feel?"

"Sad."

"What a big cast you have."

"It is big." She pointed and said, "All my friends signed it. See."

"Oh wow. That's neat."

"It's hard to walk with it. I get to use crutches."

"Oh, my! How did it happen?"

"I fell down in my ballet class."

"I bet your teacher felt bad about that."

She hung her head and went back to playing with her doll. "Yeah."

"What is your teacher's name?"

"Mrs. Daley. She's a really nice lady."

"I bet she is," he said as he got to his feet.

"I'm sorry about your father."

She got very quiet. "Thank you."

She looked down and stroked Barbie's hair. Tears rolled down her cheeks. "You'll get the man that did this and put him away forever, won't you?"

"I'll try."

"Do you promise?"

"Yeah. I hope your leg gets better real soon. Have a nice day."

He never liked making promises because he knew that the case would probably not be solved. If the perp was caught, a defense attorney might get the person off on a technicality. The irony was jarring. In his former life, Seth might have done precisely that.

Debbie heard him approach the door and slipped into her bedroom down the hall. She peered out and saw him going toward Michael's room.

Music was blaring. Logan knocked, but Michael didn't hear him. He knocked a bit louder and shouted, "Michael, it's Detective Logan. I need to talk to you."

The volume decreased and Michael stuck his head out a crack. Strands of light brown hair were hiding his blue eyes. "Oh, it's you."

"I need to ask you some questions."

"Go ahead," Michael said as he led him into the room.

Logan looked in fascination around the room. Posters of action figures slaying dragons hung on the walls. There was hardly any space left. Snapshots from family trips were pinned to a bulletin board by his bed. There were a lot of pictures of the kids on amusement park rides. There was another one of him in a Little League uniform. Ribbons and metals were pinned on the wall. A skateboard was leaning in the corner by the door. Michael went over to his stereo on the bureau and turned it off. Logan pulled a chair to the foot of the bed and sat facing the boy.

"You were the last one to see your father alive, is that right?"

"Yeah."

"What time was that?"

"About eight. He was in the shower when I went down the street to play video games with my friend Jeff."

"Did you see or hear anything unusual?"

He shook his head. "No, we were really into the game and couldn't hear anything. Then my Mom called and I went home."

"How did your father act that night?"

"How do you mean?"

"Did he act nervous or preoccupied?"

He thought carefully before answering. "He yelled at me."

"What about?"

"I don't know. I think he was mad at my Mom and just took it out on me."

"Why was he mad at her?"

He shrugged his shoulders and said, "I'm not sure."

"Did he ever fight with your mother?"

He hung his head and said, "Sometimes they argued."

"What did they fight about?"

"Money...it was usually about money. And sometimes I heard them fighting about Raymond. I don't think they knew I could hear them. I don't think my father liked him much."

"Did they have a fight that night?"

Michael fiddled with his shoestrings and said, "Yes."

"Did anyone come to the house before you went to your friend's house?"

He shook his head.

"Did your father seem uptight or nervous a few days before this horrible thing happened?"

"Not really," Michael said slowly. "But he did seem kind of... distracted...just before he went fishing that weekend."

"When did he go?"

His voice rose. "Just before it happened. He left on Thursday afternoon and got home late Sunday night. And then he went to work on Monday morning, and when he got home—somebody killed him." He rubbed his eyes and looked away so Logan wouldn't know he was crying.

Logan looked around the room and pretended he didn't notice. He looked back at the bulletin board and trained his eyes on snapshots of the boys holding fishes. Metals and ribbons hung below them. He pointed to one of the pictures and said, "That's some fish you've got there. Shad, right?"

Michael sniffed and said, "Yeah. I caught it when I was nine. I think Peter's ego was bruised."

"I bet you know about all kinds of different fishes."

"Yeah, I do." His face drooped again. "But my dad knew more. And he even knew the best places to go too."

"Oh really?"

"He caught a Swordfish once."

"You don't say."

"He stuffed and mounted it. We used to have it hanging up in the den. It's at our cabin now. He used to do all kinds of deep sea fishing. But then he got busy. We used to go camping every weekend. Sometimes we climbed mountains. But I liked fishing the best."

"It sounds like you guys had a lot of fun."

"It was a blast! But then he got really busy. We didn't get a chance to be with him much at all when he was working. He was hard to get close to. He kept at a distance. When we were together– it seemed like he was going...overboard."

"He was overcompensating. Maybe he felt guilty for not spending so much time with you guys."

"Maybe."

"Divorced parents often feel guilty. Did you know they were thinking about getting a divorce?"

"Yeah, we knew. Peter told me."

"You two seem close. Do you look up to him?"

"Yeah, he's great! But don't tell him I said it."

Logan grinned and said, "I won't."

"I don't want him thinking that I look up to him."

"He's like a father figure, right?"

"Sort of."

"Because your father was always busy with work, except for a weekend trip once in a while?"

"Yeah. But they weren't that often."

"Did you always listen to Peter?"

"I guess."

"Did you see a tan van parked outside when you went to your friend's house?"

"No."

"Why do you think your father acted preoccupied last weekend?"

"He said he was really bothered about a case he was working on."

"Did he mention what it was about?"

"No."

"Thanks for taking time to talk to me. I'll let you get back to what you were doing."

Logan went out of the room and the music was blaring again. He jotted notes and went back downstairs. He went back into the family room to talk to Peter, but the boy had gone off with a friend. He headed out to his car and slipped behind the wheel.

Debbie peered out of her bedroom window and watched him pull onto the street.

✻   ✻   ✻

CHAPTER 5

Logan headed out to Broad Meadow to talk to Peter Molloy. The drive out to the boarding school offered a pleasant distraction from the stress of cracking homicide cases. He watched as the rolling meadows slipped by, and could not believe that there was such a great distance between houses. He was used to cramped living spaces city life offered. He slowed down when he approached a hill that twisted into a hairpin curve. The road was so narrow that no one dared pass a motorist. When he stopped at a traffic light, one of very few in the area, he covered his nose to avoid catching a whiff of manure from a neighboring farm.

"It's certainly not Philly," he muttered.

He crossed the intersection and slipped past a farmer driving his tractor at five m.p.h. on the highway. Logan pulled around a bend and drove into the entrance to the old school. A year earlier, he had spent a lot of time on the campus, investigating the death of a popular basketball player. The tragedy affected the lives of students and faculty alike. He had made such a nuisance of himself, he wondered if the faculty would let him get out of his car when they saw him coming.

He drove past the old stone archway at the entrance with its cobblestone walkway tucked underneath pine trees. The Student Center could be seen a short distance from the archway. It was a one-story brick building with a steeple on top. At one time it could have either been a church or a one-room schoolhouse. The historic marker stood nearby, with a sign next to it in bright red letters that proudly boasted that Broad Meadow was founded in 1885. Everything about the campus advertised its age in a positive way. The Episcopal church with its massive steeple pointing skyward greeted motorists as they drove down the entrance road. For over a hundred years, students lived in the grand Victorian house across the street from it. It was a beautiful afternoon and girls hung out on the front porch, or they sunned themselves on the second floor deck.

Logan glanced at the girls lacrosse team practicing, then turned right onto a tree-lined lane that led into the main campus. The late afternoon sunlight that trickled through the dogwood and Cherry Blossoms were a magnificent sight. To the right, boys stripped down to their shorts and lay on blankets, next to girls who had on tank tops and bikinis. Other kids sat on the dock and dangled their feet in the pond. It was too nice a day to be inside.

Hullien Hall loomed on the right. The large stone building was one of the oldest structures on campus. Logan drove past it and veered to his left. He pulled into a parking space and headed toward Stewart Hall. This modern two-story brick building seemed dull in comparison to other ones on campus, but the young men who lived there didn't care. It offered freedom from nagging parents.

The potent stench of fertilizer drifted from a nearby farm. Wherever he went, Logan could not escape that foul aroma. He pinched his nose and walked hurriedly into the building. He went to the student lounge and saw boys on a couch studying and watching TV. He asked them some questions about Peter and found out which room he was in. He went down the hall and a tall, strapping boy standing under a backward baseball cap went by him.

He smiled and said, "Can I help you, sir?"

"I'm looking for Peter Molloy's room."

"I'm his roommate, Todd."

"Then maybe you can answer a quick question. Where was he the night his father died?"

"We were cramming for a test that night."

They stopped halfway down the hall and Todd opened a door on the right. They went inside and Logan saw Peter sitting at his desk, studying. He had on a matching sweat shirt and pants with the school's logo emblazoned on them. He couldn't wait to get out of the school uniform and dress comfortably when the final bell rang. Todd grabbed a notebook and quietly went out of the room.

Peter looked up from his notes and said, "Oh, hello, Detective Logan. I'm sorry that I skipped out the other day. Can I help you?"

Logan pulled up a chair and said, "I need to ask you some questions. I believe there is more to your father's murder than we originally thought."

"I thought he just snuck up on a burglar and got hit on the head."

"That's what somebody wants us to think, but it isn't the case."

Peter eyed him quizzically and said, "What do you mean?"

"I can't say right now. Let's just say it was suspicious. I'm sorry to have to ask you these questions. I know it's hard for you now, but I have to ask. Where were you when it happened?"

He looked at Logan in disbelief and said, "You think I did it? I was here studying for a test."

"I always ask people where they were when a crime has been committed," he explained. "I talked to some of your dorm mates and they said you had been acting upset a few days before it happened. Some of them overheard you get into an argument with your mother on the cell phone. They said you wanted to talk to your father. They said that you seemed nervous."

"So what if I was? My mom said some things that bothered me. What else is new?"

"What did she say?"

"It's none of your business."

"You don't like it here."

"It's that hard to figure out?"

"You don't like the rules."

Peter rolled his eyes and grunted. "A moron could figure that out."

"I can't blame you for being angry. All of a sudden you're the man of the family."

"Who says I'm angry?"

"Well, you look like you've got an attitude problem. It's a wise ass, don't come near me or else attitude. I'm not falling for it."

"Yeah, I've got an attitude only because I'm pissed off with things."

"I had an attitude when I was your age."

"Don't give me a story about how things were when you were my age."

"What are you pissed off about?"

"I don't have to tell you anything."

"My father was a cop just like me. He was killed in the line of duty. I was pissed off because some dirt bag shot him."

Peter raised his right eyebrow. He struggled for the proper response but said nothing.

"I was twelve at the time," Logan said after a long silence. "The same age as your brother. I was angry at the world for a long time. My grandfather raised me."

"What about your mother?" Peter asked reluctantly.

"She was killed in a car accident a couple years later."

"That's rough, man."

"Tell me about it. I gave my grandfather hell. But we eventually got over it. I learned so much from him." He glanced at the bulletin board over Peter's desk. His eyes trained on a snapshot of Peter holding a Striped Bass. "So, you like to fish too? My grandfather loves to take me out fishing."

"I love it. We used to go fishing at our cabin on the lake."

"Where is it?"

"In Maryland."

"It sounds nice."

"It's beautiful this time of year."

"I bet it is," agreed Logan. He leaned forward and asked, "What are you pissed off about?"

"A lot of things."

"So why did you want to talk to your father so badly? Did you want to talk to him about getting you out of this school?"

"You could say that," he grumbled.

"How do you get along with your brother and sister?"

"All right."

"Did you resent them for getting more attention from your father, now that you're here?"

Peter leaned back in his seat and said, "Yeah, while I rot here in this rat hole, my dad paid all kinds of attention to them."

"I take it that he never did that when you were little."

He rolled his eyes and gave Logan a sideways glance. "No, he was too busy establishing his career. Then, when I was older, he spent 'quality time' with us! We used to go fishing, but then I got too old for it I guess. That's when he enrolled me in this wonderful school, if you can call it that. Then he took them places when my football team played at away games. I was irritated that they couldn't have worked out times when I could have gone with them. They all went to the cabin, while I was stuck here."

"I'm sure it wasn't intentional."

Peter groaned. "Well, it seems that way to me. Every time they all went on those trips, Michael always got to go fishing with my dad. Sure, I felt left out. Of course I'm angry. I felt like my Dad didn't want me around. I wondered what I did to make him so mad? I thought I must've done something to make him mad enough to send me away. Maybe he just wanted to get away from me. Maybe he resented me."

"Maybe he wanted you to get a good education."

He rolled his eyes and said, "Yeah, right."

Then Peter burst into tears. Logan patted his shoulder to calm him down.

"I can't stand it!"

"I know you won't believe it when I say it'll get better," Logan said gently. "You've had a major shock and you've got to take care of your family. It's a big responsibility."

"It isn't fair!" Peter shouted through tears.

"I know. Life isn't fair."

"Why did this happen?"

Logan looked sadly at him and said, "I'm upsetting you. Why don't I come back another time?" He apologized for bothering him and headed back to the car.

*　　*　　*

It was getting dark when Logan pulled up to his apartment building. He loosened his death trap of a tie and marched toward the entrance. He passed Mrs. Ferguson on the steps and grinned at her. She was carrying grocery bags. He offered to help carry a couple and they engaged in small talk as he followed her into her apartment. He put the bags on the kitchen counter and they continued their chit chat.

"How is the Seth Molloy case?" she asked.

"It's challenging," he admitted.

"Do you have any leads?"

"Not at the moment."

"I know, you can't talk about it.

He smiled and said, "Something like that."

"I understand." She sighed and said, "It's such a tragedy."

"I know."

"It's so sad for the children to lose their father at such a young age."

He nodded and said, "I know the feeling."

"Oh–oh, that's right. I'm sorry."

"It's okay."

"How's Penny?"

He beamed. "She's just great!"

"I haven't seen her lately."

"She's busy at work."

"The next time she's in town, bring her over to see me." She leaned forward and grinned. "Better yet, why don't the two of you have dinner with Gus and me? Just give me a call the next time she's here."

"I'll do it," he replied amiably. "It sounds like fun."

"How's spaghetti?"

"I can't wait."

They continued chatting until he politely excused himself and went to his apartment. He leaned down to pick up his mail by the front door and went into the living room. He tossed it on the coffee table and went into his bedroom. He threw his tie on his bed and peeled off his clothes. He went into the bathroom and took a long, hot shower. Then he turned off the spigot and dried off. He went over to the bureau and smiled at the framed photo of Penny wearing the Santa Claus hat. Next to it, there was a gold framed childhood picture of him with his grandfather that was taken on a fishing trip. They had on fishing getups and were holding rods. A framed picture of his mother at the beach when she was in college hung on the wall by the window. Next to it, was the last picture of him with his parents. In between them, there was one of Frank in his mother's arms when he was six months old.

He changed into more comfortable clothes, a t-shirt and shorts, and went into the kitchen to get a beer. He went back into the living room and plopped on the sofa. He turned on the TV, checked messages, then attacked his mail. A few bills, but mostly junk that wound wind up in the trash can.

The living space was cramped. The kitchen was smaller than cramped, but he didn't mind. He wasn't there enough to notice. Except when Penny made an occasional visit. They made the most of it. They cared about seeing each other more than what it looked like inside his apartment.

Penny knew what she was getting when she went out with him in the first place. He was a man of simple means. The only thing that mattered was that he had a place to stay, and food to eat. His entertainment center consisted of a twenty-four inch TV, a stereo, and a laptop, old VCR tapes and DVDs. Most of his furniture was of the thrift store variety. Some of it was there when he moved in, some of it came from his old apartment in Philadelphia. Potted plants on the window ledge were Penny's contribution.

His living room walls were adorned with memorabilia from his former life. He proudly displayed his Police Academy diploma next to the one his father earned several years earlier. Their awards and medals figured prominently next to each other. On the opposite wall, there was a portrait of Francis in uniform with the American flag behind him. Framed snapshots of Frank's friends at the Townsend Police Department hung next to it. There were pictures of Joe and Harry horsing around at the station. There was one of him behind bars. A photo of Stan Green wearing a black robe in the morgue, clowning around as the Grimm Reaper added a certain macabre touch. Another personal favorite of Frank's was one of bartender Debbie Turner mugging it up for the camera with Townsend's men in blue at their favorite Friday night hangout, Barney's Bar and Grill.

He channel-surfed, but there was nothing on that interested him. It was either reality or game shows, or political news programs. He settled for a documentary about ancient Egypt on the History Channel, and propped his feet on the coffee table.

He couldn't help but think about the Molloy kids. He was the same age as Michael when he lost his father too. His thoughts flashed back to the day he found out that his father had been killed in the line of duty.

He was in Mrs. Wilson's Social Studies class when the principal came in and went over to her. He whispered something to her and then they scanned the room to look for Franky. He remembered the look on his teacher's face. A moment earlier, she appeared happy and jovial, as she launched into a discussion about the geography of South America. A genuine look of fear and sadness flashed in her eyes now. She pointed to Franky and asked him to go out in the hall with them. He gathered his book bag and slowly got to his feet. He knew something wasn't quite right. Normally when a kid was called out of the classroom there would be an announcement on the P.A. system. Why did the principal come in? He would never do that.

She instructed the students to read a section in their text books, and put her arm around Franky's shoulder as they exited the room.

He looked from the principal to the teacher, his eyes wide with alarm. "What's wrong? You're scaring me!"

Mrs. Wilson wiped away tears, too stunned for words. Mr. Holland stepped in and said, "Oh, Franky. I'm so sorry to have to tell you this. Your father...your father has been injured in the line of duty."

He eyed him quizzically. "Injured? How?"

Mr. Holland rubbed Franky's shoulder and said, "He was shot."

Franky leaned against the wall and looked up at the older man. "He was shot? When—when did it happen?"

"About a half an hour ago," he said calmly.

"Is he...is he okay?"

He looked at Mrs. Wilson. She slapped her hand to her mouth and drew a deep breath. Tears rolled down her cheeks.

"He was rushed to the ER," reported the principal. "Oh, Franky. He—he didn't make it."

Franky could have only imagined what his classmates must have thought, when he let out a bloodcurdling screech when they broke the bad news.

"Noooo!" he shouted. "Noooo!" He burst into tears, suddenly feeling lightheaded.

He flew into the larger man's arms, and Mrs. Wilson wrapped her arms around them. He stood there shaking.

Mrs. Wilson ran her fingers through the boy's hair and said, "Oh, Franky. I'm so sorry. Your father was such a nice man."

"You need to go to the office right now," Mr. Holland said. "Your mother will be there to pick you up soon."

They stood on either side of him and escorted him down the winding corridor. His legs felt rubbery and they had to help hold him up.

When they wound up at the office, Mrs. Wilson sat with him while they waited for his mother to get there. She spoke softly, offering words of comfort. He was so out of it, that he had no recollection of what they were talking about, years later.

He might have forgotten what his teacher told him, but what happened when his mother arrived would forever be stamped in his memory. She looked God-awful. She hadn't taken time to comb her hair. It was matted and in her eyes. She had on sweats and moccasins. She didn't even take the time to put on a coat. They stood there hugging each other, crying buckets. She rested her tear-stained face against his, and sobbed uncontrollably.

"Oh, Franky," she managed. She squeezed her eyes shut and spoke incoherently. All he could get out of her was, "We'll get through this."

They thanked Mrs. Wilson and Mr. Holland and slowly wove their way out the front door. She had double-parked in the fire lane but didn't care. No police officer would dare give her a ticket on the day Francis Logan was shot.

The telephone rang, jarring him back to reality. He muted the TV and leaned over the end table. He picked up the receiver, happy to hear Penny's voice.

"How are you doing?" she asked.

"I'm kind of tired. The Molloy case is keeping me busy."

"Is there anything you can tell me?"

"Right now, we're looking for a guy that was seen leaving the house about the time Molloy was killed."

"Do you think he did it?"

"I won't know that until we can talk to him."

"Well, good luck finding him."

"I'm tired of thinking about the case. What's up with you?"

"Are you doing anything this weekend? I thought I'd come by."

"That would be great!"

"All right. I'll come after work."

"Okay. I'll see you then."

"I figured you could take a break."

"Baby, you're just what I need."

They were so busy talking, that he lost track of time. They had been talking for an hour. The bird wall clock chirped at ten o'clock.

He rubbed his hand through his hair and said, "It was really good talking to you. I'll see you Friday night."

"Bye-bye."

He hung up and stared at the TV screen. There now a documentary about alien conspiracy theories. He fell asleep with the remote control in his hand.

✻ ✻ ✻

CHAPTER 6

Dazzling Interiors was sandwiched between the barber shop and the Army Recruitment Center on Main Street. Before and after posters of rooms that Debbie and Raymond transformed were prominently displayed in the bay window. After years of struggling, happy clients spread the word, and their company took off. Now there was often a backup and Debbie had to turn customers away.

Nancy Ryan could not make up her mind. She slowly flipped through the thick pattern book and jotted down the swatch names and numbers that she liked, while Debbie offered suggestions.

"I think your best bet is to go with navy blue for the living room walls," Debbie said. "It would go well with the patterns for the sofa and chairs."

"It's so hard to decide. There are so many nice patterns."

Debbie smiled. "Take your time. I want you to be happy with your decision."

Ten minutes later, Nancy had still not made a decision. Debbie opened her portfolio and showed her before and after photos of homes she renovated. Nancy settled on three designs that she liked the best. Then Debbie helped her decide which curtains would look best. About a half an hour later, Nancy left pleased with her decision.

Debbie finished filling out the paperwork, and went over to the bay window that overlooked Main Street. She put the swatch books on their hooks and sat back at her desk. She drew a preliminary sketch of Mrs. Ryan's living room and checked her calendar. The next day, she would go to her house to take measurements.

She gazed out the window, lost in thought. She was not looking forward to the funeral. It was so unfair that the children had to go through something so horrifying at such a young age. She was so emotionally distraught, she hoped she was making the right decisions. She had no frame of reference about this sort of thing.

Her family would be there, but they were not much comfort. Her parents had always been supportive of everything she did. That changed the day Seth came into her life. Her father took an immediate dislike to him. Months later, when the subject of marriage came up, David and Ellen begged their daughter not to marry him. Debbie's brother and sister sided with their parents. Her older sister Rae was blunt. Seth was manipulating and controlling. Little brother Tony warned Debbie to be careful. Marrying him would be the biggest mistake of her life. Debbie wouldn't listen. She was blinded by love. She couldn't see his numerous faults and married him anyway.

She fell for his charm and magnetic personality on their first date at a Sushi bar and grill in Philadelphia. His eyes lit up when he spoke about his career. He had to be a smooth talker to be a successful attorney. She admired his take charge attitude. He ordered for her. He politely asked for his order to be taken back to the kitchen.

Little did she know that was Seth's pattern. He started off nice, but could be a monster at times, in a subtle way.

He was an immensely private man and never opened up to her if something was bothering him. There was something about him that she couldn't put her finger on. Something dark and mysterious. If something happened to him in his past, she could not get him to talk about it.

She respected his privacy and stopped prying. She found it odd that Detective Logan was learning things about him that she didn't know. Maybe Seth wanted it that way. She wished she had listened to her family years ago. If she had, she wouldn't have her three wonderful children.

That was one positive thing that came out of her miserable existence with that man.

She continued sketching Mrs. Ryan's living room layout to keep her from thinking negative thoughts. Her mind took her to places she didn't want to go. She focused on the events leading to Seth's murder. She thought about their argument before she left for the restaurant to meet Raymond. She wondered where Seth got the photos of the two of them? What if he had copies? What would Detective Logan think if he found them?

Raymond Sinclair spent the morning measuring and cutting wood in the back yard of Steve and Betty Johnson's home. He wiped sawdust off his goggles and laid another piece of plywood on the saw. He slowly moved the blade across the wood, while the unusable section fell on the grass. He turned off the saw and sat on the porch steps for a well-deserved break. He reached for his thermos and gulped down his water. Then he dried perspiration off his forehead with a handkerchief. Temperatures were reaching seventy-eight degrees and it was only eleven o'clock. He had been at it since seven. He was getting too old to do this alone. He often thought about hiring an assistant, but he didn't want to have to pay someone else to do something he had done his whole life.

His bones creaked when he got back up on his feet. He went over to his wood piles and carried planks, two in each arm, into the family room. He spent the rest of the morning putting up the boards for the family room addition. Large fans blew sawdust in the air. His mask was layered in it.

He had always liked being his own boss. He could make his own hours. He could take off whenever he wanted. He liked the independence. He didn't like having to practically grovel at Seth Molloy for another loan. It was humiliating. What he hated most was that smug look Seth got on his face, a few hours before his demise. It was his air of superiority that angered Raymond. Seth had no right being a father. Though Raymond had no kids of his own, at his age he knew he would make a better father than Seth Molloy. Now he would have a chance to be a step-father, if Debbie would come to her senses and agree to marry him.

He never considered himself a family man. Right now, he was trying to show interest in what the younger kids were doing, but it was a considerable effort. He came off as controlling, but he had to be, knowing what they had to deal with. Seth was a monster.

Raymond's father was just as much of a control freak. He always drove the car. He handled the finances. He worked late into the night, and seldom spent time with the family. Vacations were usually unpleasant. His parents, Raymond, Sr. and Meg were mismatched. They often argued. Finally, Meg had enough and divorced him. She got a job as a receptionist, with regular hours, and was always there when the kids came home from school. His father kept his distance. They only saw each other on special occasions and holidays.

The oldest of three children, Raymond, junior kept his younger siblings in line. He had several jobs when he was in high school and dropped out after his first year in college. He worked at construction sites, and went on to work for a master carpenter. He survived many layoffs during harsh economic times and always managed to get back on his feet. He always found work eventually.

He had sensed Seth's growing anger toward him. Two romantic rivals didn't mix well, especially when both men were equally domineering. Raymond knew that they came from different worlds but didn't care. He had always loved working with his hands. He was thrilled to make houses look better. He enjoyed looking at the expressions of happy clients when they first saw the results of his backbreaking labor.

Seth was not accustomed to dirtying his fingers. If anything had to be fixed, he called whoever could take care of the problem. He was the classic workaholic who spent many long hours hovering over law books and talking to accused criminals on a daily basis. He lived and breathed crime. At least he decided to put criminals away, rather than take a lot of money to get them back on the street.

Seth Molloy won the prize in the control freak category, though. Raymond couldn't understand why Debbie didn't leave the man years ago. She was a saint to have put up with him this long. It was time to put her years of anguish behind her. Seth wasn't around anymore. It was time to think about the future. If they got married, it would be a solution to a lot of problems. He would take care of Debbie and the kids. She could help him out of the financial spot he had just gotten himself into recently.

About three thirty, he wiped a bead of sweat from his forehead and drank water from his thermos. He worked for another couple of hours and packed his equipment into his truck. The family room addition was showing progress. He slipped behind the wheel and pulled down the road. Little did he know it that he was being followed...

✻ ✻ ✻

CHAPTER 7

Logan examined the contents of the wallet that he found on Seth Molloy's bedside table.

"You can learn a lot about a person by looking through his wallet," he said.

"And their trash," Lieutenant Winters added.

"That's funny."

"What?"

Logan handed him a snapshot taken about twenty years ago. "That's Molloy, but it isn't his wife and kids."

"Didn't you know?"

"Know what?"

"He was married before."

"You never said anything."

"You didn't ask."

"Maybe she might know something."

Harry shook his head and grunted. "That's doubtful. They went through a nasty custody suit and she skipped town. He charged her with kidnapping their two kids. It was in the papers for months."

"Damn!" Logan cried. "I spent hours online looking at old newspaper files."

"I guess you didn't look far enough back, my friend."

"I was just a kid at the time. I was too busy rounding up my buddies to go play football with. I don't remember a thing about it."

"It got ugly," he said as he exited the room.

Logan reached across the desk for Townsend's newspaper, the *Times-Sentinel* and read articles pertaining to the Molloy case. He detested reading anything to do with a case he was working on. Two out of three times the article was inaccurate or out and out wrong. At least his name was easy to spell. The only thing the reporter could get wrong was his rank. Responses from friends and colleagues were typical. Molloy was a pillar of the community and could do no wrong. Well, obviously someone out there hated him enough to murder him. Logan whistled when he saw the size of the obit. It took up one and a half columns. The head and shoulder shot was from a decade or two ago, when his hair was naturally dark. Not only was Molloy an outstanding lawyer, he also devoted free time to helping the community. The list of accolades was numerous. The funeral was going to be on Friday morning. He was about to fold up the paper, when a name caught his eye.

"Mr. Molloy leaves behind a wife, Amelia, and a son, Robert, and a daughter, Sarah, from a previous marriage." He jotted the names in his pad and continued reading. The rest of the clip mentioned Debbie, and his three children from his current marriage.

He leafed through the paper and noticed a small side-bar on the third page, with a two paragraph blurb that detailed the events surrounding the ugly custody suit that resulted in Amelia kidnapping their children. He whistled and shook his head in disbelief.

He jotted a note to do a Google search on it, and went down the street to get something for lunch.

Debbie wrapped her arms around Bonnie and wiped her tears as pallbearers carried Seth's casket past them. Participants included courthouse employees, judges, and lawyers. Police in their dress uniforms took up several pews. She pulled herself together for her children's sake. After the service, motorists followed the hearse to the cemetery.

Logan held his umbrella firmly in his hands as he joined the mourners in the crowd. Raindrops bounced off the umbrellas and made it difficult to hear the minister talk. His eyes trained on Peter. He was the picture of strength. He seemed to be very much in control, despite the fact that he was wearing a suit and tie that seemed alien to him. It was on so tight, he kept loosening the knot. Raymond Sinclair patted Debbie's shoulder to help calm her down. Tears streaked down Bonnie's cheeks. Michael held his little sister's hand. His expression was stone-like.

After the graveyard service, Logan expressed his condolences to friends and family members. He shook Debbie's hand and said, "I'm so sorry, ma'am."

"Thank you," she said.

"I'll find out who did it."

When he moved to the end of the line, he chatted with colleagues. He glanced over and saw a tall slender brunette standing by a tree away from the group. She was clad in a black outfit with a matching scarf and dark sunglasses.

Their eyes met. She smiled and continued watching. She wasn't smiling at him. She seemed happy, not grief-stricken.

He approached her, but she merged with the crowd and vanished from view. When the crowd thinned, he saw Peter on a bench next to a tree, crying. His face was buried in his hands.

As Logan walked back to his car, his thoughts flashed back to the day he found out that his father had been killed in the line of duty. He was about the same age as Michael. The grief was the same.

When the events surrounding Sergeant Francis Logan's death came to light, it didn't matter to his wife and son how it could have been prevented. He was dead and wasn't coming back.

The funeral was at a large cathedral in Philadelphia. There were so many mourners in attendance, folding chairs had to be put in the back. A lot of people stood in the doorways. Others couldn't get in and stood in the narthex. The room was crazy with men and women in their uniforms.

Francis's colleagues were so kind. They came up to them, one after another and offered their support. It was at that moment, that Franky's dream of becoming a cop just like his father grew stronger. At the reception after the service, Vera and Franky heard many colorful stories about Francis. Some were true and others were juiced up or sanitized for the kid's sake, Franky was sure. It was their kindness that made Frank the compassionate man he was today.

☆   ☆   ☆

CHAPTER 8

P enny Lane's parents assured her that she wasn't named after "The Beatle's" hit song, but she had her doubts. She was tired of acquaintances humming the tune to her namesake. After a while, she stopped telling people she met what her last name was. But the day she met Officer Frank Logan, she had to tell him everything.

Everyday, he walked past the neighborhood coffee house on Market Street, and checked her out when she was hanging out with her friends. When he reached the corner, he would turn around and watch her all over again.

He was drawn in by the light that emanated from her dark eyes. She talked with her hands, the sign of an expressive woman. Her features were soft and delicate. She had a heart-shaped face and a slender figure. Little did he know the affect she was going to have on him.

Their stories about how they met differed, depending on who they were talking to. He claimed that he bumped into her, innocently enough at the coffee shop. He spilled coffee on her or something like that. He was more like a stalker in her version. The truth was something in between.

He memorized the name and make of her car. One day, he stopped her on a routine patrol. She was forced to pull into a gas station parking lot. He didn't have to pull her over. It just gave him an excuse to talk to her. When she was forced to hand over her licence and registration, he looked dubiously at her and asked if it was a fake name. Was she an underage woman trying to get into a bar? She assured him that that was really her name, and he tried not to laugh.

She put up a major fuss. He had no right pulling her over. She hadn't done anything wrong.

He was too busy flirting with her to pay attention to what vehicular laws she might have violated.

The conversation ended in a warning and a date at the coffee shop that she frequented. He grinned and hoped she had a nice day.

Since his move to Townsend, he did not get to see her as often. Occasional weekend visits were not enough. She usually came to see him, because he didn't have time to get back to Philly.

He felt totally wired with anticipation as he wandered about the apartment waiting for her arrival. He showered and shaved, and spent quite a while looking himself over in the mirror. He put on an obnoxiously red checkered shirt and slipped on his blue jeans. Then on went the cowboy hat and boots.

He practically flew across the room when he heard a knock at the door. Penny stood there all smiles and threw her arms around him. He took a quick glance at her hair. It was shorter than he would have liked. Her color of the moment was light brown. She had on tight jeans and a t-shirt that had the words "Born to Have Fun" on it.

He kissed her and said, "You look great, honey."

She winked and said, "So do you."

They talked for a few minutes, then headed out to meet his friends.

It was a typical Friday night. Frank and Penny joined the gang at Barney's Bar and Grille.

It was nice to unwind with friends after attending Seth Molloy's funeral a few hours earlier. Debbie Turner was clowning around with members of the Townsend police department. Patrons sat at bar stools and watched the baseball game on a gigantic TV screen. A Brad Paisley song blared in the background. The Phillies game drowned it out. It was so loud, it was hard to hear each other talk.

"Did you have any luck finding the tan van?" Frank asked Harry Winters.

He shook his head and grunted. "You know you're not supposed to talk about work here, Frank."

Joe Flosky couldn't have agreed more. "You can talk about it, but we won't listen to a word you say. Got it?"

"Sorry I brought it up."

Joe craned his neck and grinned dumbly at the young blonde four tables away. Trying not to be obvious, he looked back at his friends.

Harry winked and said, "There's a girl for you."

"She didn't draw back in fear this time," Logan agreed.

Penny slapped Frank's shoulder and said, "Be nice."

He grinned and said, "That was me being nice."

"Why don't you go for it?" suggested Harry.

"It's worth a shot." Joe got up and sauntered over to the woman, while his buddies watched.

Joe leaned down and beamed. Then he grinned and they all smiled back, trying not to laugh out loud.

"What do you think he's saying?" asked Harry.

Frank leaned back and stretched out his arms over his head. "Probably some lame line."

"I hope he doesn't use that worn out phrase of his."

"You mean the one that goes like, 'I'm here to protect and serve at your beck and call?'"

They exchanged knowing looks. Harry nodded his head and said, "Yeah. That one."

Penny leaned forward and said, "I think you're being too hard on him. Give him a break."

"I've only been here for a year and the guy's had a lot of girlfriends," Frank said. "Maybe he should try a different approach."

Harry took a long swig of beer and said, "He ain't too smooth in the lady department, if you know what I mean."

"I think he's a sweet, unpretentious man," Penny said. "He's a real gentleman. Not like the jerks I see at clubs in the city."

"And how often is that?" Frank quizzed her.

"How I spend my nights is none of your business, Detective Logan," she answered sharply. "If you would spend more time with me, then you'd know."

Harry burst out laughing. "She's got you there, Logan!"

"Well, maybe I should get to Philly more often then."

"Maybe you should."

He leaned in and kissed her.

Megan Winters gushed and said, "Awl, isn't that romantic?"

Harry squeezed his wife's hand and said, "He learned everything from me."

"I hope not!" quipped Megan. She sprang to her feet and slapped his arm. "Come on, let's dance!"

Harry groaned and did as she requested. They flapped their arms to and fro like drunken fools on the tiny dance floor. Frank and Penny laughed and pointed at them.

Joe came back to the table with the blonde and said, "Guys, this is Mary."

"Hi Mary," they said in unison.

She beamed and said, "It's nice to meet you all."

"She's from the big city too," he explained. "She's here visiting her sister."

Penny grinned and pointed to Frank. "I'm visiting my boyfriend."

Mary squeezed in between them and Frank ordered another pitcher of beer. When the music stopped, Harry and Megan rejoined them. After another round of introductions, the old married couple greeted her with open arms. Mary's sister, Katie, joined them and didn't seem to have any trouble fitting in. They were so busy talking that they lost track of time. About two hours later, Katie glanced at her watch and said she had to get up early for work. They promised to come back on Saturday night to watch a local country band perform.

When they were gone, Joe nodded and grinned dumbly at his companions. "There goes the future Mrs. Joe Flosky."

"Well, I'm glad you to hit it off," Megan said. "I hope it works out this time, sweety."

"What she's trying to say is, don't screw it up this time," Frank chided.

Penny slapped him again. "Frank, you're so bad!"

"I'm naughty. Not bad."

"Well, you know what happens to naughty kids," Penny said. "They don't get presents from Santa."

"Then I won't get any presents this year."

Harry changed the subject so he wouldn't vomit on himself. They talked about fishing and hunting until last call.

☆　☆　☆

CHAPTER 9

Peter couldn't believe all the nice things people said about his father at the funeral. Newspaper reporters painted him out to be a saint. He helped with many charitable organizations. He could do no wrong. Peter thought he was a domineering ogre.

He couldn't concentrate on his Biology notes. He gazed out the window and watched classmates laughing as they darted across the parking lot. It looked like they were having a good time. He wished he could be that lighthearted. Years of being in the middle of his parents hellish fights forced him to grow up fast. He was more serious than kids his age, and it was harder to fit in.

He immersed himself in his studies so he didn't have to think about his troubled family life. He was a model student. He made good grades. Teachers admired him for his hard work. He was a fine athlete. Classmates looked up to him. No one would have ever guessed what was really going on inside his head. He was physically fit, but not so fit on the inside.

He hated being a role model. He just wanted things to be normal at home.

His father made a decent living as a lawyer. They lived in a nice house, in a nice neighborhood. Peter went to a fancy boarding school. But with all that, no one would ever guess the misery that went on inside the house. They all learned to cover up their family secrets so well, they didn't know who they were anymore.

He resented his father for the anguish he caused. Peter had always thought about getting him back.

His thoughts were interrupted by the loud footsteps his roommate made when he entered the room.

"What's wrong?" Todd asked.

"Nothing. I'm just uptight about the Biology test."

"I don't think it's just about the class. Losing your dad's rough, man. Do you want to talk about it?"

"Not now."

"Okay, well, you know where I'll be, right?"

"Thanks, Todd." He looked back at his notes and continued studying.

Four days after the night out with Penny and his colleagues, Logan sat in his car, eating a roast beef sandwich while waiting for Raymond Sinclair to come out of the dry cleaning store a half a block away.

"The joys of surveillance," he sighed. "What's taking him so long?"

Logan hid behind a newspaper when he saw Raymond exiting the building. He was carrying a suit wrapped in plastic. He unlocked his car door and hung it on the hook. When he pulled out, Logan followed him. He was headed west of town.

Sinclair's errands were mundane. He made quick stops to the bank and the post office. A little while later, he pulled into an apartment building spot and got out. He pulled out the suit and slung it over his right shoulder. He went into the building and came back ten minutes later, empty-handed. He looked in the detective's direction, but didn't see him. He got back in his car and drove out of the town limits.

They were now on hilly back roads. Motorists unfamiliar with the unexpected twists often got into accidents.

Logan whistled and said, "I know where you're going, Sinclair."

The race tracks loomed on the right. Logan pulled onto the shoulder and saw Sinclair drive into the entrance. He waited for five minutes, then found a spot to park on the grass across the road from the race grounds.

It was a beautiful day to spend at the races, Logan thought as he approached the gate. It was a balmy seventy-four degrees, and there were no dark clouds in the sky. He wound his way onto the bleachers and saw Sinclair leaning against the rail. He went up to him and tapped his shoulder. Raymond flinched when he looked up at him.

"Well, funny seeing you here," Logan said. His words were drowned out by the roar of the crowd and the galloping horses. The announcer's voice droned in the background, describing the horses movements in every detail.

Realizing there was no point in talking, Logan just smiled and waited for the commotion to die down.

"And the winner is "Lucky Lady!"

The crowd was a buzz with exhilaration.

When it quieted down, Logan made his move. "Fancy seeing you here."

"What do you want Logan?" he grumbled.

"Seth's secretary told me you asked him for a loan a couple of times. A few hours before he was murdered, you went to him begging for more money. He wouldn't help you out and you got into an argument with him. Is this where all your money winds up? Does Debbie know?"

Sinclair snarled and said, "What I do on my own time is nobody's business."

"It is when it involves company money."

"You can't prove it."

"Well, it's just a theory. How much money did you lose at the tracks?"

The look of dismay that shot across the man's face revealed that he had just lost a pretty penny. Sinclair brushed past him and said, "I don't have to tell you anything!"

Logan walked hurriedly to catch up with him.

Raymond waved his hands in the air and shouted, "Leave me alone!"

"I think I can pretty much guess what happened. You used company money to pay back your gambling debts."

Sinclair pretended he was deaf and merged with the crowd. A few minutes later, Logan saw him walking past a long line of people standing at windows ready to place bets. The fear and apprehension in the man's eyes were palpable. He stopped to wipe a bead of sweat from his forehead. His shirt was soaking wet. He stumbled like a drunk man toward the exit.

Logan went back to Debbie Potter-Molloy's house about four o'clock the next day. She opened the door and said, "Hello, Detective Logan. Do you have any leads?"

"Yes, but I can't say anything until I know more."

"I understand."

She led him into the den and he saw Raymond Sinclair on the reclining chair. Raymond lifted his head from the newspaper and glowered at him as he entered the room. Debbie offered Logan a cup of coffee. He accepted and took slow careful sips. Logan looked back at Debbie and said, "I just need to review some of the facts. You were both eating out that night?"

"We were at a Chamber of Commerce dinner at the Garden Terrace restaurant at six o'clock," she said.

"What time did you leave to pick up Bonnie?"

"About eight thirty. Well, actually, I left about an hour before that. I went to my office first."

"Were you alone?"

"Yes."

"Where were you, Raymond?"

"I stayed to talk to prospective clients at the restaurant. I left about seven thirty and went home."

Logan looked back at Debbie and said, "So you picked your daughter up on Main Street and got home about nine o'clock?"

"Yes, but what does that have to do with anything?"

"You were alone for about an hour. It takes about ten minutes to drive from your office to your house. That would have allowed plenty of time to get to your house, kill Seth and slip back out to get your daughter."

"I don't like what you are suggesting."

"I'm sorry, ma'am. I'm just trying to cover all the bases."

"Maybe you should spend more time looking for who killed my husband and leave us alone."

"You're right. I'm sorry I brought it up." He checked his notes and looked back at her. "When I did the room search, I noticed that you and your husband had separate bedrooms. Why?"

Debbie closed her eyes and put her fingers on her temples. She looked back at him and said, "He worked late hours. He often didn't get in until after midnight. He–he didn't want to wake me up so he slept in the guest bedroom."

"How often did he do that?"

"More than I would have liked," she admitted.

"Were you having marital problems?"

"We had some problems. We were just never able to get them worked out."

"What kinds of problems?"

"I don't see how that is relevant to the case."

"It could be. I need to know as much as I can about your husband if I'm going to find out who did this."

She closed her eyes and drew a deep breath. "Okay. I was extremely unhappy and–and asked him for a divorce."

Raymond Sinclair chewed his fingernails and eyed Logan suspiciously.

"Were you seeing someone else?" He looked over at Sinclair.

"You might as well know the truth," she said. "I was miserable with Seth. I felt trapped being married to him. I wasn't in love with him anymore. It was unfulfilling. There was a lot of apathy in the marriage. It was just like spinning wheels. When Raymond and I started to have feelings for each other, I knew there was no way to fix my broken marriage. Seth couldn't accept the fact that I loved another man."

"Did you act on your feelings?"

"We wanted to," Raymond confessed. "But I thought it was a trick. I told her that Seth could hire someone to take our pictures together and that he could use it against her when she filed for custody of the children."

"We had to be careful about everything we did," she added.

"Were you lovers?"

"We didn't sleep with each other–I couldn't risk it. But we were very fond of each other. When you work that closely with someone for so long, you tend to get closer. I think Seth was jealous that Raymond was so much a part of my life."

"I bet he was." Logan reached in his jacket pocket and pulled out the picture he removed from the manilla envelope in Seth's office file cabinet. He waved it at them and said, "This picture proves otherwise."

She gasped and put her hands over her face. "Where–where did you get that?"

"There are other ones just like it at his office."

Raymond snatched it out of Logan's hand and said, "Let me look at it." After careful scrutiny, he said, "It was obviously Photoshopped. Look at the halo around my hairline. It looks like my face was pasted on someone else's body."

"Well, you have a good eye. But if it would have held up in court, that's a different matter."

Raymond could not have disagreed more. "It can be easily disqualified. All I have to do is remove my shirt to prove that man isn't me."

"Did you know about the pictures, Mrs. Molloy?"

"Of course not!"

"Well, it's just a thought."

"I don't like what you're driving at, Detective," Raymond said angrily.

"It looks to me like Seth had damaging evidence that he could have used against you in a custody hearing. And you couldn't take that chance."

"They're fake!" she insisted. "We didn't sleep with each other!"

Logan glanced back at Sinclair and said, "I think Seth resented you so much that he refused to give you the loan for your business endeavor, isn't that so?"

Raymond chewed his nails. After a moment of silence he said, "Yeah. He was so jealous of me, that he wouldn't even help out his wife. He refused to help us."

Logan turned his attention back on Debbie. "Did he have a life insurance policy, Mrs. Molloy?"

"Yes."

"How much was it for?"

"That's none of your business." She looked at Raymond, then back at Logan. "It is enough to put our kids in Ivy League universities. We won't have to worry about anything, I should say."

Logan looked at Raymond and said, "It sounds like it is enough to pay the debt, Mr. Sinclair."

"It was at that," he agreed. "But it wasn't motive to kill him. That is what you are implying, isn't it, Detective Logan? It's an insult! I wouldn't marry her just for the money she'll get for Seth's life insurance money."

"I'm sorry you feel that way Mr. Sinclair, but I have to ask these questions," Logan answered sharply. "Did you know about the insurance policy?"

He nodded and looked out the window.

"Now, to get back to the divorce problem," Logan continued. "Did you serve him with the papers Mrs. Molloy?"

"No, I just told him I wanted a divorce."

"When did you tell him?"

She burst into tears and sobbed. "Just before I left to meet Raymond at the restaurant. It was--it was the last time I saw him alive!"

"How did he react?"

"He was angry," she said through her tears. "He refused to give me the divorce and we got into a nasty argument."

"Is that how the photo of you and Seth got ripped up?"

She wiped her face and nodded. "When I started for the door, he--he–grabbed my arm real hard and--and I told him he was hurting me, but he wouldn't let go! I had to pull free and that's when–"

"You ripped your dress?"

"Yes," she said blubbering.

"So you were lying when you said you ripped it on the door going out of the house, correct?"

"Yes."

"You wouldn't have said anything about the ripped sleeve if I hadn't mentioned it the other night, correct?"

She looked away again and said, "I didn't want anybody to know."

"You're upsetting her!" Sinclair cried. "It was a robbery plain and simple. One of the guy's caught Seth by surprise and killed him."

Logan talked over him. "I know it's hard to talk about, but it's important. I'm sorry ma'am, but this has to be done. Your husband died under suspicious circumstances. I'm going to need to get a DNA sample from you."

She waved her hands in alarm and said, "What do you mean? A burglar hit him on the head! What is so suspicious about that?"

"Detective Logan, you should spend more time tracking down the burglar than harassing this poor woman!" Sinclair thundered.

"I'm just trying to explore all possibilities, sir. Debbie admitted arguing with Seth prior to his murder. Maybe you came home early from dinner, Mrs. Molloy. Maybe you hit him on the head. It's just a thought."

"You're way off base, Detective! But if I do it, maybe you'll leave me alone."

"It's just procedure, ma'am. I'll make arrangements for you to give us a sample."

"It's an invasion of privacy!" Raymond exclaimed.

"I'm sorry. It has to be done."

"All right, let's get it over with," she said. "You don't know how foolish this will make you look."

"Maybe it will," Logan agreed. "But we have to know. I'll let you get back to your quiet time alone. If you'll excuse me."

He left them alone. On his way out he heard her say, "Do you believe the nerve of that man?"

"It's unbelievable!" Sinclair cried.

When Logan got back to the station, Captain Ward went over to them and asked, "What have you found out?"

Logan gave him an update, and then handed him the private detective's business card he found in Molloy's wallet. "Maybe this guy can give me some answers."

"Well do something. Mrs. Molloy has been calling me up and pressuring us to find out who killed her husband."

The captain went back to his office. A short time later, Joe Flosky went over to Logan's desk.

"Did you find out anything about the drifter?" Logan asked.

"Not a thing. How about you?"

Logan clapped his hands and said, "Yes! It turns out that Raymond Sinclair spent too much time at the race tracks and lost his pants."

"So what do you think?"

"At the moment, he seems to be the most likely suspect. He knew about Seth's life insurance policy. And when he found out that Debbie wanted a divorce, he couldn't let that happen because he knew that Seth might get angry and cancel the policy. If she divorced him, that would be that. I think Raymond was so desperate that he had to kill Seth to keep the money supply going. And he knew the layout of the house too. All we need is some hard evidence."

"I hate to break it to you pal, but he was at the restaurant with a lot of people."

"I know, but he was alone when he left the restaurant. If he left at seven thirty, he had plenty of time to go to Seth's house, hit him on the head, mess up the furniture to make it look like a burglary, and exit without being seen, minutes before Debbie returned."

"Mrs. van Horn is pretty sure that she heard the car engine backfire about eight o'clock," Flosky added. "And we all know that it must have been the gunshot she heard, because she saw the drifter fleeing the Molloy residence and driving away in the van right after that. I suppose she could've been wrong about the time she heard the noise."

Logan grunted his agreement. "I'm just wondering about Debbie Molloy."

Flosky looked at him in alarm. "You think she hit him on the head?"

"Well, she admitted that she was unhappy in her marriage. And they were arguing before she went out to dinner that night. She ripped her sleeve. And there were compromising pictures of her with Raymond."

Flosky's eyes lit up. "No kidding!"

"He left a copy of them in his office file cabinet."

"It makes you wonder."

"Exactly. Seth could have used those against her during the custody hearing."

"She would have lost the kids for sure."

"Which would be the perfect motive for murder."

Debbie leafed through a *Better Homes and Gardens* magazine, but nothing stood out. Her mind was elsewhere. She was haunted by the events that unfolded after finding Seth's body. Instead of calling the police right away, she helped Bonnie to her room. She couldn't let her little girl see her father that way. She felt guilty that she didn't call the police after helping Bonnie settle in for the night. She had made a beeline for Seth's office afterward. She knew he hid the drawer keys in a mug on the bookshelf. She had yanked open the drawer and rifled through files. Her eyes fell on the manilla envelope, and she snatched it out. She dumped the contents on the blotter. What to do with them? The police would find them. She slammed the door and gathered the pictures together. She fed them in the shredder, one after another, tears streaking her cheeks. The trash can soon filled with a myriad of strips of colors. Then, she pulled out her cell phone and called the police. She went down to the kitchen to get a trash bag and hurried back upstairs. The police would be there soon. She didn't have much time. She poured the contents into the trash bag, tied it, and hid it in her S.U.V. She had just gotten to the porch, when she heard sirens screeching down the street. She turned around and saw three squad cars pull onto the curb. What happened after that was a blur...

The telephone rang, jarring her back to reality. It was a pushy salesman. She hung up gracefully, and went over to get another cup of coffee and sat back at her desk. Her thoughts automatically reverted back to the compromising photos that Detective Logan found in Seth's office file cabinet. Now he wanted to get her DNA sample!

She continued taking notes for Mrs. Ryan's living room. The bell over the door jingled and Debbie looked up to see Detective Logan enter the office followed by criminalist Jim Anderson. He was of medium build with a blond crew cut and a pale complexion.

"Good morning, gentlemen. What can I do for you?"

"I need to get your DNA sample," Anderson said.

"All right, but it's a waste of your time."

"That might be, but it's procedure, Mrs. Molloy," Anderson said.

He collected her sample and apologized for the inconvenience.

"You should track down the burglar and take his swab," Debbie suggested.

"We will as soon as we find him," Logan said. "Nice place you've got here. Have a nice day."

They started out, when Logan paused and turned around. Jim Anderson waited by the door.

"One more thing, Mrs. Molloy."

She looked incredulously at him and said, "What?"

"When I searched your husband's study, I found a strip of paper on the floor, but I couldn't put it together. It felt like photo paper. Then it dawned on me. Your husband did have copies of those incriminating photos, didn't he?"

Debbie tried to maintain an even expression but was sure that she wasn't pulling it off. "I don't know what you are talking about."

"The shredder had a few loose pieces that you didn't pull out," he added. "Here's what I think happened. Hours before he died, you two argued. You got so upset when he showed you the pictures, that you started screaming at him. It's just a thought."

"Well, you thought wrong. We were arguing about the divorce."

"I put some of the pieces together and saw what looked like a part of a face. You must've panicked when you realized that the police would search his study. You knew you had to get it out of the house before we arrived. What did you do with it?"

Debbie remained icily quiet.

"I suspect that you hid it in your car. It doesn't matter. I can get a search warrant."

"It won't do you any good," she said. "It's gone now. The trash collector picked it up already."

"Ah, so you admit hiding it."

"All right, so what? Of course I didn't want you to find it. I was afraid of what you'd think. It's like I said. Raymond and I didn't sleep together. I had to get rid of it. I didn't want people to think the wrong thing."

"You have to admit, ma'am, that it does look rather suspicious. It makes you look guilty."

"I was angry," she admitted, "but I didn't kill my husband!"

Logan smiled and said, "Well, it's just a thought. I'm sorry that I upset you, ma'am. Have a nice day."

He followed Jim Anderson out the door. She scowled as she watched them walk past the office. She turned her attention back to jotting notes on furnishings that would look nice in Mrs. Ryan's living room.

*   *   *

CHAPTER 10

Luke Springer was a gruffy private detective in his late forties. With two failed marriages behind him, a third divorce was pending. Either he left his wives angry or they left him angry.

He spent too much time at the office, doing things private investigators do to crack a case. When he wasn't doing that, he spent time at local taverns, arriving home in the wee hours of the morning, smelling of cigarette smoke and beer. He was behind in his case load, and his desk was cluttered with piles of folders and newspaper clippings for cases that had gone unsolved. Desperate family members came to him as a last resort.

He leaned back on his swivel chair, blowing cigarette smoke as he talked on the telephone.

Logan sat across from him, patiently waiting. He had been trying to reach the man for several days, but every time he called, the messages were full. He was probably staked out in his car, taking pictures at ungodly hours of cheating spouses.

There was a framed black and white picture of Springer hanging on the wall. It was taken a long time ago. His hair was jet black then, and he was half the size he was now. Years of drinking and smoking resulted in a beer belly and a smoker's cough. Now, there was no trace that he had had dark hair.

Springer hung up and snapped, "What do you want Detective Logan? I'm really busy."

"I'm investigating the Seth Molloy homicide."

"Oh that?" Springer raised his right eyebrow. "What do you want to know?"

"I found your business card in his wallet. I've found out some things through my investigation. I know he had a lot of enemies. And I found this death threat in his trash can." He handed him a copy of it and said, "What do you make of it?"

"Isn't it obvious? Somebody was trying to kill him and succeeded."

"So you don't think it was just a random killing by a burglar either?"

"Somebody was doing a number on him."

"Is that why he hired you?"

"Among other reasons."

"Why else would he have hired you?"

"Initially, he hired me to follow his wife's business partner. He was overprotective of her. He didn't trust the guy, for good reasons. He spent a lot of time at the racetrack."

"And he lost quite a bit of money," Logan added.

Springer smiled wryly. "You're good."

"But to get back to the death threats. When did this come up?"

Springer blew smoke at the ceiling and looked back at Logan. "It had been going on for some time. Molloy had been getting notes and crank phone calls for about six months. The nut job had something on him and was threatening to expose him."

Logan looked eagerly at him and said, "Did you find out what that something was?"

"I never did. Molloy was a private man. It was hard working for the guy. I had to practically pull teeth to get him to tell me things. So that's why I pulled myself from the case."

"He got crank calls?"

"Somebody changed the refrain of *American Pie* to *Today'll be the day that you die.*"

"Really?" Logan jotted it in his pad. "Could you get a trace on it?"

Springer shook his head and grunted. "It must've been from a pay phone."

"Is there anything else you can tell me? His wife desperately wants to find the person who killed him."

Springer leaned back in his swivel chair and puffed away on his Marlboro. "If you want to know some things about him, talk to his ex-wife."

"Where is she?"

"He didn't know. That's why he hired me in the first place. She split town after a brutal custody case. He did some smooth-talking and painted her out to be a lush. He got the kids and she took off with them one night. It was as if she just dropped off the face of the Earth. He charged her with kidnapping the kids. I wouldn't be surprised if she wasn't in some way responsible for his death."

Springer scratched his beard and met Logan's gaze. "There was no love loss between them. Maybe she hired a hit man to kill him. That doesn't make sense, though. If she's lived this long wherever she is, it doesn't make sense that she'd hire somebody to kill him. Eventually the trail will lead back to the person that hired the hit man."

"Maybe she changed her name."

"I spent months checking various government databases and came up flat. It was as if she vanished into thin air."

"Can you give me a list of all the places you checked?"

Springer chuckled and said, "If you want to. It's a long list. It'll take a while."

"That's fine."

"I'll make copies and you can stop by in a day or so to get it."

"Thanks." Logan shook his hand and headed out.

Logan went back to the police station and got online. He did another Google search on Seth Molloy, and checked files from twenty years ago.

A headline read: "MOLLOY CUSTODY BATTLE HEATS UP."

TOWNSEND--"Don't let him near the children!" shouted a desperate Amelia Molloy after learning that her husband Seth would gain custody of their children.

In what has become a grueling five month custody suit, Judge Warren G. Robinson awarded custody to their father, defense attorney Seth Molloy, on Wednesday afternoon.

"I knew everything would work out for the best," Molloy said after court. "When things started to get ugly, Amelia made me out to be a horrible person."

Mrs. Molloy claimed that Seth was prone to violent outbursts that frightened the children. She appeared agitated when Judge Robinson ruled such statements unsubstantial due to lack of evidence.

At that point, Amelia Molloy lost control and shouted, "He'll hurt the children! There's no telling what he'll do."

Bailiffs escorted her out of the courtroom. Her father, Thomas R. Smith, of Townsend, rushed to comfort his frightened daughter...

Logan clicked on an article from a Philadelphia newspaper. The headline read: "SCARED MOM FLEES WITH KIDS; DESPERATE DAD WANTS ANSWERS."

TOWNSEND–After a five month battle in divorce court, local lawyer Seth Molloy gained custody of his children, only to have them snatched away from him two days later, by his ex-wife, Amelia. She has been charged in connection with their kidnapping.

"I just got out of the shower and went to check on them," Molloy said. "When I went to their rooms, they weren't there. She was really upset at the trial. She's the only person I can think of who would do such a thing. If she brings them back, I'll drop the charges, and we can work some things out..."

Logan opened his desk drawer and pulled out the telephone book. He ran his finger down the endless SMITH entries.

"Jeez, why did it have to be Smith?" he groused.

At long last, he found the number for Thomas R. Smith, scribbled the address and paid the old man a visit. He strolled up the walkway and rang the bell. There was no answer, so he rang again. Then he knocked. He was about to leave, when the door opened.

An old man peered out the screened door and asked gruffly, "What do you want?"

Logan held out his badge and introduced himself. "Mr. Smith, I need to ask you some questions in reference to–"

"Seth Molloy's death," he answered for him. "I knew it would come to this."

Smith opened the door and looked down the street in both directions. He let Logan in and didn't say anything. He shuffled across the entryway, Logan at a careful length behind him to catch him in case he fell. Logan figured he was probably in his late seventies. He was still able to get around without the aid of a walker, but had one handy, just in case he needed it. His gait was slow and unsteady. They went into the den, and Smith eased into a rocker. Logan pulled up a chair and sat near him.

A framed portrait of Smith and his wife was on the end table. It didn't look like she had been there for quite a while. The room was minus a woman's touch. The curtains were dingy.

"I need to talk to your daughter," he began.

Smith grumbled and said, "You don't need to talk to her."

"Please, sir. It's important. I need to ask her questions about the custody suit. I'm trying to get as much information about Molloy as I can."

Smith rocked on his rocker and was quiet for a long while. "I'm surprised the bastard wasn't killed years ago," he said at last.

"He could have just been in the wrong place at the wrong time, but I still need to know as much as I can about him. He wasn't killed in a random attempted burglary. Someone made it look like he died defending his house."

"I'm not really surprised," Smith said. His eyes seemed vacant.

"I need to talk to your daughter. I thought she might know something. What is her address?"

Smith stiffened and continued rocking. Logan repeated the question.

"I have ways of getting information you wouldn't like," Logan said. "I have to get at the truth. My search has led to you."

"You won't get anything out of me."

"You're a bitter man. You hated Molloy for the pain he caused your daughter. Maybe you killed him."

"The thought has crossed my mind, every so often," Smith said. Then his hands twisted into a gruesome position. "As you can see, my gnarled hands make it impossible for me to do much of anything. Sure I've thought about doing him in. But why drag up the past? I'm an old man. Molloy had twenty years to think about what he did. That's punishment enough. Now, he has finally received his death sentence."

Logan leaned forward and asked, "What exactly did he do?"

"One night, he beat her so bad that she had cuts and bruises all over her face. He had a fierce temper. She caved in, as always. She said she fell down the steps. He was establishing himself in his career, and she didn't want to embarrass him. He probably got to her. People who are abused will do anything to survive, I suppose. He brainwashed her. I tried to help her, but it was no use. She turned me away and refused to listen."

"Where did she take the children?"

He clammed up.

"Did you help her leave town?"

Smith awkwardly wiped tears with a Kleenex. The paper shook in his unsteady hands. "It was the only thing a father could do. If I hadn't, I'm certain that he would've killed her.

She feared for the children's safety. He was so smooth in the courtroom. He could convince people of anything. He was a snake! He could use his good natured fatherly crap to win over the judge.

No one would have ever believed he was capable of such horrible things! He was an upstanding defense attorney. If people only knew what kind of animal he was!

"The papers painted him out to be some kind of super dad, always doing things with the family. Taking them fishing and camping. He could lie through his teeth, that's for sure. He could be believed, just by using his wit and charm. That's what she fell for. He was a charmer, that's for sure. And I can see how Amelia, or anyone for that matter, could have been taken in by him. I felt like vomiting every time I saw write-ups about the charitable things he was doing to help the community. Charity my ass! My wife and I warned her not to marry him, but she refused to listen."

"Where is she?"

"I wouldn't be surprised if somebody killed him on purpose," Smith said gripping his cane with his good hand.

"Quit stone-walling!" Logan demanded. "If you're worried about her being arrested, we can work things out. I'm sure the statute of limitations has probably run out by now."

Smith stared blankly at the detective.

"What are you covering up?"

"I'm not covering up anything," the old man insisted.

"I realize that you're protecting your daughter, Mr. Smith, but it won't work. I'll get a search warrant if I have to."

"I'm an old man," he protested. "Leave the past alone."

Smith's resistance made Logan more curious. What was he hiding? There was a long, uncomfortable silence as both men, young and old, stared each other down. It was a stalemate.

Logan knew that by the time he came back with a search warrant, Thomas Smith would destroy the evidence. There had to be a way to get him to cooperate. He wasn't leaving till he did.

Logan was the first to break the silence. "I know that you don't want Amelia to go to jail. I get that. But Seth can't hurt her anymore. By now the statute of limitations has run out."

Smith regarded him skeptically. "How do I know you aren't lying like the police did when you were probably walking around in diapers?"

Ignoring the crack, Logan changed his tactic. "We can make a deal. You can call her. I can talk to her. I don't have to know where she is."

"Phone calls can be traced," Smith pointed out.

"That's true, but it's just you and me here. Nobody else."

Smith scowled at him. "I'm not buying it."

"It's in Amelia's best interest to come forward. I imagine that living life on the run for this many years has taken a significant toll on her."

There was another long, uncomfortable silence. Thomas Smith gazed out the window, deep in thought. Then, he looked back at the detective and stared into his eagle-like dark eyes. Maybe he could trust him. He was willing to give it a shot.

"Okay, I'll give you some addresses she used to be at. I suppose that wouldn't hurt anything."

Logan drew a deep breath and said, "Now we're getting somewhere."

"You can look around, but don't expect me to help you," Smith said.

"I didn't expect you would."

Smith was rocking on the rocking chair, working the New York Times crossword puzzle. Logan was rummaging through piles of papers on Smith's desk in the corner. He went over to the fireplace and studied the framed photographs on the mantle. He saw one photo that was similar to the one he found in Seth Molloy's wallet.

A boy with light brown hair was on a dock, proudly holding up his prize. The fish was so big, he had to hold it in both hands. Logan picked up the picture and went over to Smith.

"When was this picture taken?"

"About twenty years ago."

"Have you had contact with them since Amelia left town?"

"Not as often as I would have liked. But she preferred it that way."

Logan went back to the desk and rummaged through drawers. There was an envelope with stacks of photographs in it. He thumbed through them and stopped when he saw a more recent photograph of Thomas Smith with the boy from the other picture. He grew into a gawky looking teenager. They were holding fishes and standing next to a dock.

"Is this your grandson?"

"Yes."

"When was this taken?"

"About nine years ago. He had just gotten his driver's permit."

Logan pulled open the bottom drawer and found a shoe box inside. He pried off the lid and sifted through a stack of letters. There was a post card from Key West. The last two numbers of the year were crossed off with a red magic marker. The address read:

Mrs. Karl Williams
Rolling Meadows, Virginia--
May 14, –

"Dear mom, I hope you're doing well. The weather's great here in Key West. Anthony's so busy at sea, that I've had to take up scuba diving to keep busy. It's a lot of fun. I wish you were here. Love Yvonne."

"Is Yvonne your granddaughter?" Logan asked.

"Leave her out of it!" he snapped.

"When did she get married?"

"Last year."

"Where is she living?"

Smith pointed to the shoe box and said, "It's in there."

"Be that way!" Logan cried in frustration.

He flipped through more letters and closed the lid. He put the shoe box back and headed out with Amelia's address. He hoped that was where she was living now.

"Don't have a good day," Smith said.

"Likewise."

Logan showed himself out. Smith fumbled for the telephone on the end table and dialed.

"Hi honey, it's me. A Detective Logan was just here to talk to me. He's onto us."

Logan went back to the police station in a huff and sat at his desk.

Lieutenant Winters went over to him and said, "It's that bad?"

"That old man is so stubborn, it took forever for him to tell me where his daughter is. I felt like punching his lights out."

"You wouldn't do that."

"I felt like it."

Joe Flosky laughed at him from across the room. "Frank Logan: Terror to old people."

"See how you'd like it," Logan jeered.

"I know how it is," Flosky agreed. "I hate people that lie."

"People are always covering up something."

"Or covering for somebody else."

"Exactly."

"Well I have some news that might cheer you up," Winters said.

"What?" Logan asked.

"I finally got some information about the tan van."

"That's great! What did you find out?"

"The van is registered to an Adam Jones. He's our drifter. His van was spotted on a regular neighborhood patrol."

"At least something's going right," Logan said.

"It turns out Jones spent a couple of hours at the emergency room on the night Seth Molloy was killed. Get this, he told us he was treated for a flesh wound on his right shoulder."

"You don't say," Logan said.

"He matches the neighbor's description of the man she saw fleeing Molloy's house. I brought him in for questioning. He's in the interrogation room now."

☆ ☆ ☆

CHAPTER 11

Logan entered the interrogation room and saw the drifter sitting at the table. He had long sandy hair with sideburns that touched the tips of his moustache and beard. He wore a faded t-shirt and jeans with holes in the knees. His left arm was in a sling.

Logan introduced himself and pulled up a chair facing him. Lieutenant Winters came in and sat at the head of the table.

"Mr. Jones, the night Seth Molloy was murdered, a neighbor saw a man matching your description exiting his house," Logan began. "There was a bullet hole in the kitchen window. And we found a trail of blood splotches leading to the front curb. I see that your arm is in a sling. Why is that?"

"I fell off my motorcycle the other day," Jones answered cooly.

"A doctor reported treating a gunshot victim that night. And he fits your description. Bullet holes in the kitchen window match the one that the doctor extracted from the gunshot victim, which places you at the crime scene."

"I didn't do it."

"Molloy was hit on the head with a poker. His gun was found a few feet from his body. His fingerprints were on it, but he didn't fire the weapon. You and your partner made it look like a botched burglary attempt."

Adam leaned toward him and said, "I don't know what you're talking about."

"He just got out of the shower. Maybe he heard a noise downstairs while he was getting dressed. He probably confronted you in the kitchen and you dropped the loot. Your partner must've come up from behind and knocked the gun out of his hand. It went off and hit you in the shoulder. They struggled and he hit him on the head with the poker. Then he knocked some things around to make it look like a botched burglary attempt. By the time he escaped, you had already sped off in your van. You're not a very loyal partner."

"I swear, I didn't do it. You're making a mistake!"

"A few days before he was killed, neighbors saw your van parked on the street. Were you casing the joint? Were you planning to rob his house that night? Why were you there?"

Jones leaned his good elbow on the table and pressed his hand against his face. He looked at them cockeyed and said, "I was just trying to see if people needed me to do some odd jobs."

"Are you in financial trouble?"

"I got laid off about three months ago and had to go around to neighborhoods. I check out houses that need fixing."

"Where were you working?"

"I was a fork lift operator at the pharmaceutical company outside of town."

"Did you know Mr. Molloy?"

"No."

"A neighbor saw you lurking around Seth Molloy's backyard that night. Why were you there?"

"I told you. I was trying to drum up some business."

"I think you were trying to help yourself to his belongings and got shot as you fled the house. Who were you working with?"

"No one! I mean--I wasn't involved with it!"

"Do you know who he was?"

"No."

"You'd better start talking. It doesn't look good for you."

Jones sat up straight and shot an icy look in Logan's direction. "You can't prove it was me. Besides, I got shot after I left the house."

"And my dog ate my homework." Logan pounded the table. "Did you break into Molloy's house or not?"

"No!"

"Then what the hell were you doing there?"

"I was trying to get some work. I swear it."

"The bullet removed from your shoulder matched the one that came from Molloy's gun. This is your last chance to tell us your side of the story before I arrest you. With the evidence stacked against you, even the best defense attorney couldn't get you off. You can cooperate or spend the rest of your life in prison. It's your choice."

"I didn't do anything!" Jones cried. "I know it doesn't look good for me, but I tell you I didn't do it. I was at the wrong place at the wrong time."

Lieutenant Winters leaned forward and looked intently at the young man. "Then someone else did it. Did you see who it was?"

"No."

"Evidence is stacked against you Mr. Jones," Logan said. "We'll have to arrest you if you don't cooperate."

Jones ran his fingers through his long, tangled hair. "I'm telling you all I know."

"A man is dead," Logan said. "Someone killed him. We want answers. Did you see anything or not?"

"No!" snapped Jones.

"Why were you there?" Logan pressed.

"I wanted to sue the factory I worked at. I was working part time doing maintenance work around his office and getting free advice about my situation. I was going to see if he needed things painted or fixed around his house."

"Have you ever been in his house?" Lieutenant Winters asked.

"I was there once at an office Christmas party. But he wouldn't have remembered me. I was just a face in the crowd."

Logan grunted and said, "That guy sure has a nice house. I bet you were in desperate need of extra cash and decided to try burglary."

"I would never do such a thing! I swear, you've got to believe me! I never stepped foot in the house!"

Logan and Winters exchanged knowing glances.

"Your bullet wound came from Molloy's weapon," Lieutenant Winters said. "You admitted you were at Molloy's house that night. You have a van. There were household appliances scattered on the kitchen floor. You were seen fleeing the house after a neighbor heard a gunshot. Seth Molloy is dead. It can't get more plain than that."

"I've told you everything I know. Are we done here?"

"For now," Logan grumbled.

They escorted him out.

*   *   *

Two days later, Logan and his colleagues went to Adam Jones's apartment with a search warrant. They saw his tan van parked in a spot with the number 4-B on it. A red Suzuki was next to it. They approached a house with white pillars and a wrap around porch. Six mail boxes were by the door. Fire escape steps led to two second floor apartments at the rear. Another one was in the attic. The house had been converted into separate apartments to the left and right of the door. They went inside and checked the room numbers. Then they went upstairs. Jone's apartment was the second door on the right.

Adam was getting lunch, when he heard a knock at the door. He was surprised to see Detective Logan and two angry looking officers in the hall. Logan waved a search warrant in his face and he let them in.

"You have no right doing this," Adam lamented.

"We have every right, Mr. Jones," Logan said. "Your activities that night were suspicious and I want to get some answers."

Adam's eyes flashed with rage as the officers manhandled papers on the coffee table. One man went into his bed room, the other one searched the kitchen. When he opened the trash can lid, Adam screamed at the top of his lungs. "What the hell are you doing?"

"Shut up!" the officer shot back.

Adam waved his good hand in the air and watched in utter bewilderment as they manhandled his personal effects.

"I don't believe you people! You've got no right doing this! I can't believe it!"

Adam followed them into his bedroom. Logan glanced at a framed photo on the bedside table. It was of Adam and an attractive woman about his age. They had their arms around each other and were grinning.

"Pretty girl," he commented dryly. "Your girlfriend?"

Adam nodded and grunted. Logan yanked open bureau drawers and sifted through his clothes.

"Get your goddamned hands off my stuff!" screeched Adam. "I don't believe you people!"

They went back into the living room and Adam sat down. He shook his head as they continued rifling through his things. Then a short, stocky man came rushing into the apartment waving an evidence bag. It looked like ground up pieces of paper. Adam wasn't sure.

Flosky handed Logan the evidence bag and said, "I found it in the trash can out front."

Logan held it up and examined the contents. "It looks like chopped up magazine pages with missing letters."

Flosky nodded in agreement.

Adam's look of anger turned to that of fear. Logan went over and cuffed him.

"Adam Jones, you're under arrest for the murder of Seth Molloy." Then he read him his rights.

"Hello?"

"It's Adam," he shouted to be heard over the buzzing commotion in the police station. "I'm in big trouble and I really need your help."

"What's wrong?"

"I'm in jail."

"What happened?"

"They think I killed somebody. I was in this neighborhood one night, trying to get some business and somebody shot me. I panicked and ran to my van. People saw me leaving the house.

Somebody was robbing the house and dropped stuff. They think I did it!"

"Don't say a word until I get there. I'll get there as soon as I can."

"I didn't do it!"

"I'll get you out of there. Just sit tight."

Adam hung up and the officer escorted him back to lockup.

☆   ☆   ☆

CHAPTER 12

Michael Molloy hated school with a passion. He thought it was a drudgery. He felt like a prisoner there. He wished he was older and could go to school on the west coast, where it was always warm and he could be independent. He was just biding his time until he was old enough to take care of himself. He had always dreamed of splitting town and getting as far away from his parents as possible, as soon as he turned eighteen.

He knew that his parents were not getting along but didn't understand what was going on until he got a little older. He learned at an early age how adults acted two-faced. Their arguments were swept away at church, where his father laid out his charm. No one would ever guess how rotten Seth Molloy really was, or the misery his mother was feeling. No one would believe the hell that went on inside their home a few minutes earlier. No one knew how unhappy and disturbed the Molloys really were. It was all an act. They were phonies.

His mother was always smiling in public. They were told to smile and make pleasant small talk as they greeted parishioners.

When they got home, it was a totally different story. God forbid people found out their dirty little secret.

Michael had learned to steer clear of his father when he had a drink or two, especially if he lost a case. He got angry and lashed out at any family member unfortunate enough to cross his path. Peter usually got the brunt of it since he was the oldest. After he went away to boarding school, the charming Seth Molloy took out his anger on his younger son. Now Michael knew why Peter was overprotective. He felt sorry for him. He could never have any fun, because he always protected them from the wonderful Seth Molloy. It made Michael feel like puking that people couldn't see through his father's act.

All the stress and tension at home made Michael look at life differently than most kids his age. He was quiet and reserved and had a hard time interacting with other kids. He was ashamed to invite them to his house.

He was a conscientious student and didn't cause trouble. He often befriended kids who were being picked on by bullies. Teachers admired him for his hard work. Little did they know what was really going on inside his troubled mind. Jeff was the only kid that made headway with him. They enjoyed playing video games and hanging out.

For a very long time, Michael wished Seth was out of the picture. He wished his mother would dump him and marry Raymond Sinclair, whom he looked at as a suricate father. He was willing to bypass Raymond's controlling influence for a sense of normalcy.

Michael had an eye for an eye attitude. This thought had been driven into him, while putting up with the horrible things that his father did to the family. He had been thinking of ways to get back at him.

He took out his anger and frustration playing video games and with the latest gadgets. He lost track of time, slaying monsters and creatures in fantasy worlds of his choosing. He often fantasized that it was Seth's head that he blew off...

Spending countless hours chatting with online friends offered him anonymity. Anything to keep his mind busy. Anything to keep him from thinking troubling thoughts that had been swirling in his head recently. Anything to keep him from thinking of that horrible night when his father was hit on the head with the poker.

He let out his aggression on the joystick. Destroying one alien after another temporarily eased his feelings of sadness and loss. When he wasn't playing the game, he was haunted by memories of his parents screaming matches. Everybody was crying. They were all upset. There was too much tension. And then he thought about that time he ran through the woods when they were at the cabin after another major fight. He didn't know why they all went there that weekend. He hated being there with a passion.

He was rendered back to reality by a knock at his door. His mother was yelling at him again as usual. He glanced at the alarm clock on his bedside table.

"What?" he shouted.

"Come on Michael, you've been in your room all afternoon. It's almost time for dinner."

"I'm almost done!" he yelled back. "I'll be down in a minute."

Five minutes later, he ended the game and wandered, glassy-eyed downstairs. His mother took one look at him and knew he hadn't been cracking books.

"When will you ever get around to doing homework?"

"I did most of it during my free period," he lied.

"You've been playing with your games too much lately. At the rate you're going, you'll flunk out. How would you like to repeat sixth grade in summer school?"

"I wouldn't like it at all."

"Then spend more time studying and less time playing games!"

"All right, quit nagging!" he moaned.

"I know you're having a hard time right now. I get it. We all are. And–and we all are dealing with our loss in our own way." She stroked his shoulder. "But honey, you've got to concentrate on homework."

"All right."

"I'll make a deal. You can spend three hours playing your games on weekends, as long as you work during the week? Deal?"

"Three hours on Saturday and Sunday? Or three hours total?"

"Total. It's nice out. You and Jeff should ride your bikes or something. You shouldn't block yourself up in your room for hours on end. It's not healthy."

"All right," he whined. He waved his hand and marched toward the family room.

After dinner, Debbie sat on the couch with Bonnie on her lap. They were watching the Disney Channel. It was a lighthearted children's show. She turned it on late and the name escaped her.

Raymond sat on the reclining chair nearby and read the newspaper. Michael was in his room again. She could only hope that he lived up to his promise. If not there would be hell to pay.

Debbie reached to answer the telephone on the end table and said, "Hello?"

"This is Detective Logan. I just wanted to let you know that we arrested the man seen running from your house the night your husband died, Mrs. Molloy."

"What a relief!"

"I just thought you would want to know."

"I don't know how to thank you. I'm sorry I was so nasty at times. I was under stress."

"I understand. Take care, Mrs. Molloy."

She hung up and looked across the room at Raymond. "They arrested the burglar."

"That's terrific! Now we can finally get things back to normal."

When Frank reported for work the next morning, Lieutenant Winters went over to him and said, "I have good news and bad news, Logan."

"Can't I just come in and have a cup of coffee and a donut for a few minutes for once, without you giving me bad news?"

"Sorry about that."

"What did you find out?"

"That the man in the holding cell is not Adam Jones."

Logan's jaw dropped. "What?"

"The fingerprints didn't match up, so I checked the FBI database. There is an Adam Jones in the area, but he's an old man."

Logan pressed his finger to his temple and said, "Oh great!"

"The good news is that I was able to get "Jones's" real name through the prints we have on file."

"Wonderful!"

"I checked conviction records, missing person reports and FBI most wanted reports. Robert Molloy has been living under the assumed name of Adam Jones."

"Oh my God," Logan muttered.

✼　✼　✼

CHAPTER 13

Dr. Karl Williams was a spry fifty-eight-year old, who was in better shape than a lot of friends his age. He played tennis and golf, and spent two or three days a week working out at the gym. Salt-and-pepper hair and glasses were telltale signs of his age. Otherwise, he could have passed for a man a decade younger.

He had spent so much time with his nose buried in books, that life passed him by. Most of the women that he had dated earned degrees from prestigious universities, and were making significant differences in the psychiatric field. He had given up the thought of settling down and having children a long time ago. That all changed when he met Lynn at his clinic. She was not intellectually his equal, but he had gotten close to her while they worked together.

He had dealt with a lot of abused women and children, but never met anyone so frightened before. She came to him emotionally fragile. He couldn't help but want to take care of her. As their relationship developed, he gained her trust. She confessed to kidnapping her children. He agreed to keep her secret, knowing full well that he could go to jail for not calling the police. He would do anything to protect her.

He married late in life, and cherished his new role as step-father to Adam and Yvonne. They were like the children he never had. He was like the father they never had.

He had heard that Seth Molloy had remarried years ago. He hoped Seth wouldn't hurt his second wife the same way he did Amelia. He wished he could have done something to stop him from hurting her so many years ago. He often wondered what he might have done to Molloy, if they had met face to face.

When he found out that Adam had been arrested, he got up at the crack of dawn and drove as fast as he could to bail him out. He parked in a spot in front of the police station and scrambled out of his maroon S.U.V. He walked hurriedly into the station and went up to the dispatcher. "Good morning, I'm here to see my step-son, Adam Jones."

The woman gave the standard response. "I'm sorry, sir. Once someone is in custody, there is no contact with the public. You'll have to wait until they finish interrogating him."

"But I came all the way from D.C. When can I see him?"

"I'll check."

She pushed line three and spoke to Lieutenant Winters. She jotted down the interrogation room number and gave him directions. He thanked her and maneuvered his way through the station. He sat in a small waiting room, and watched police personnel wander in and out.

Donald T. Jenkins hovered over stacks of files pertaining to the Seth Molloy murder investigation. He was a large man in a fancy suit. He spent more time reading legal documents and less time exercising. He was at least two hundred fifty pounds. Pockets of fat collected at his neck. His cheeks sagged from the weight. His fingernails were yellow from years of smoking.

He glanced back at his client. Adam was so nervous it looked like he was about to jump out of his skin. He assured him that everything was going to be all right and looked back at the documents.

About ten o'clock, Logan entered the interrogation room and introduced himself to the attorney. He spread crime scene photographs across the table. There were close up images of blood splotches leading from the kitchen door to the driveway and the bullet hole through the window. Another one showed a wide angle shot of the loot on the kitchen floor.

"These blood splotch pictures prove that you were at Molloy's house the night he died," Logan began.

Jenkins looked stone-faced at him. "You have conducted a sloppy investigation, Detective Logan. You've built your case on circumstantial evidence and you know it." He pointed to the photo of the loot on the kitchen floor and said, "According to my notes, no stranger's fingerprints were found on these appliances."

Logan wasn't having any of that. "That might be the case, Mr. Jenkins, but his prints were on the kitchen doorknob. My officers and I have talked to neighbors up and down the street and they were in agreement. They said a man matching your client's description was in the neighborhood about the time of the murder. One woman saw him running out of the house."

"My client says he was just in the wrong place at the wrong time."

"We were quite thorough in our investigation."

"It's an open and shut case. You couldn't find a suspect, so you nailed poor Adam. Now let's go through your investigation, one step at a time." He sorted through the photos and pointed to a close up shot of the poker. He placed it next to one of Seth Molloy's body. "According to the crime scene report, there is no physical evidence linking my client to the crime. Fingerprints were not found on the poker. Molloy's fingerprints were on the gun. Lab tests proved that he didn't fire the weapon. Try explaining that away, Detective Logan. Any judge that presides over this case would dismiss it in a heart beat. And as strange as it seems, I really do believe Adam was at the wrong place at the wrong time. The murderer made it look like signs of a struggle and tossed the loot in the kitchen. Then he fired shots through the kitchen window to make it look like a failed burglary attempt and Adam got caught in the crossfire."

"I find it hard to believe that Adam just happened to show up at the house and Molloy wound up dead. There are a lot of unanswered questions. Start talking."

Adam glared at the detective. "I didn't do it."

"Your mother was charged with your kidnapping twenty years ago and you have been living under the assumed name of Adam Jones ever since." Logan leafed through the piles and handed Adam a copy of the death threat. "Your father was planning to meet with a private detective to investigate death threats that he had been getting." Logan opened his briefcase and removed the evidence bag with the cut up magazine pages in it. He shoved it toward Adam and said, "That's funny, this proves otherwise. Letters matching the ones on the death threat came from these magazines that we found in your trash."

Adam rested his face on his hand and said, "So? It doesn't prove anything."

"It proves that you sent the death threats."

"You're really going over the limit Logan!" snapped Jenkins. "Don't say another word Adam."

"It's all right, Mr. Jenkins," he said. "If I don't tell him every-thing, we'll be here all day." He looked back at Logan and said, "I sent them. But I swear I didn't kill him. I just sent them to scare him a little bit. That's all."

"Now we're getting somewhere," Logan said. "Were you also responsible for the crank calls? You know, the one's with the lyrics, *Today'll be the day that you die.* It sounds like a threat to me."

"I had nothing to do with that."

"But you know who did, don't you? Maybe your mother knows who did it."

Adam pounded the table and shouted, "Leave her out of it! I'm telling you, I don't know who did it!"

"I've been checking phone records. It's only a matter of time before I find out the truth. If you've been holding back, I won't be a happy camper. Who's your partner?"

"I wasn't working with anybody I tell you! When I got there, somebody shot me."

Logan pointed to the photos and said, "There were household appliances on the floor by the back door. Right near the window that was shot. Right where you were standing."

Adam scratched his head, deep in thought. "Wait a second. You keep saying that. But–but, I didn't see anything on the floor."

Logan shot him a puzzled look. "You didn't?"

Adam's face brightened. "I didn't see anything in the kitchen."

"Which proves that he was at the wrong place at the wrong time," Jenkins was quick to point out. "It means that the burglar shot him after he killed Molloy. Adam's blood splotches were found on the door-knob and on the grounds, not inside. There is no physical evidence that Adam was in the house. Maybe if he had gone into the kitchen, he'd be a dead man. It's iron-clad proof that my client didn't do it."

"Or so he says. Did you see who did it?"

"No. I couldn't see beyond the kitchen."

"Did you go in the house?"

"No, I hadn't gotten in yet. I was standing in the doorway."

"Why were you in back? Why didn't you go in front?"

"I rang the front doorbell but there was no answer, so I went in back."

"So you decided to pay him a surprise visit for old time's sake," Logan commented dryly.

Adam ran his right hand through his matted hair and said, "I wasn't sure how he'd react after all these years. I thought he might not want to see me. I didn't want to scare him."

"Where is your mother now?"

"Please don't drag her into it."

"Your father was hit on the head. Where is she?"

Adam stroked his beard and silently rehearsed what he would say next. "She's been in and out of Rehab for years."

"Is she there now?"

"I don't know."

"Did you always do things for her?"

"I had to. She was too sick to help herself. At one point, I was taking care of all her financial affairs. Sometimes she would lie in bed for hours. One year, the house was almost foreclosed on. She has days when she looks right through you and doesn't seem to know who you are. It's as if she's in a fog. It's from all the drinking. Seth drove her to drink. She can't help you."

"How were you all able to live on the run for all those years?"

"It was hard, but we managed."

"She must've been really scared to take off with her own kids like that after your father gained custody."

Adam rested his head on the table and played with his hair. He looked up at Logan cockeyed and said, "It was a nasty divorce. I was just a kid at the time and I don't know much about it. We were on the road for years, moving from town to town. I couldn't make friends easily. I'd start to get close to them and we'd have to leave again. When I was in high school, my mom expected me to be the breadwinner. I had to help out. But that changed when she married Karl. We couldn't stand each other and I split when I was sixteen." He glanced over at the two-way mirror, hoping that his step-father was watching and said, "Sorry, Karl."

"Where did you go when you ran away from home?"

"I headed out to California. I got into using drugs...and I was always in between jobs. That's when I got into trouble with the law."

"And the police never traced your alias?" Logan asked.

"I guess I was lucky that they didn't check."

"How did you end up back here?"

"I grew up. I knew I had to get back on my feet again. So that's why I went back to my father's house. I wanted to borrow some money."

"Did he actually talk to you?"

"He didn't want to have anything to do with me."

"That must have made you angry. I bet you got so angry you killed him. You could've worn gloves."

"Don't say a word," Jenkins advised. "That was uncalled for Detective Logan."

"You can say what you want Detective, but I didn't do it!"

"Maybe your mother was so upset about what he did to her, that she sent him the death threats." He leaned forward and said, "Where is she Adam? If you don't tell me, I'll do some digging myself."

"All right. She's been in Pine Meadow Hospital for three months. It's outside of D.C."

"Maybe she wouldn't mind having a visitor."

"Leave her out of it!"

"What name is she going by these days?"

"Mrs. Karl Williams," Adam said sarcastically.

"Come on!" Logan snapped.

"Answer the question," Jenkins said.

"Lynn," Adam replied angrily.

"Now we're getting somewhere," Logan said. "Did your mother ask you to do things for her?"

"I felt obligated," he said. "It was something I felt I had to do. She was down and out before she met Karl. We struggled to survive every day. That isn't unusual. When I got my act together, I came home and I got a job. I'd visit her in the hospital and give her checks to help pay the bills."

Logan leaned forward and looked intently at him. "How did you feel when your own father rejected you?"

Adam looked at Jenkins for suggestions.

"You don't have to answer that," the lawyer told him. "He is only trying to get you so upset that you'll say the wrong things."

"So you did a lot of odd jobs when you got your act together?" Logan asked.

Adam rolled his eyes and said, "Yes."

"What did you do for money?"

"We survived somehow," Adam admitted.

"So you never once thought about going to your father for financial assistance?"

"No!" the veins stuck out in Adam's neck. "Not after what he did to her."

"You can't tell me the thought never occurred to you."

"Well, it would have been nice if he had been there for us. But that would have been impossible under the circumstances."

"Twenty years ago, he put out a $100,000 reward for information on the abduction of his children," Logan said. "Unfortunately, no information was available. Sadly, two decades passed without a clue. He gave up after years of searching and became a bitter man."

"He had some more kids to take his mind off things," Adam said in a sarcastic tone.

"True, but he never forgot," Logan said. "Can you really forget your own children?"

"I wouldn't know. I don't have any kids."

"Me neither," Logan said. "But Amelia Molloy did. She was so desperate to get you away from your father, that she risked everything. She changed her name and identity, and always lived in fear of her shadow."

"She never told me why we changed our names," Adam said. "I was only seven at the time. It's kind of foggy. A lot happened. Later, after she married Karl, I was looking for something in her bedroom dresser and came across a letter to her father. She told him that she changed her name to Lynn Jones. But everything was always a big secret. I think she was afraid he'd hurt us if he found us."

"That sounds like sufficient reason for killing him," Logan said. "Maybe he caused her so much pain that she asked you to do her a favor."

"No, it wasn't like that!"

"So you're saying you killed him?"

"No! You're putting words in my mouth!"

"Then what do you mean?" He waved the death threat in Adam's face. "What about this?"

"Come on, Detective Logan. Leave my client alone. Can't you see that he's had enough of your idiotic questions?"

Logan gathered the photos and put them back in the folder. "I'm done for now, but I am going to find out who you were working with."

"How many times do I have to say it? I was in the wrong place at the wrong time. I wasn't working with a burglar, I swear."

"The truth has a way of coming out," Logan said. "And sometimes it isn't pretty."

He escorted them out of the interrogation room, and took Adam back to his cell.

When Logan went back upstairs, he saw a man in a navy blue polo shirt and tan Kackis sitting across from his desk. He introduced himself and said, "Can I help you?"

"I'm Dr. Karl Williams. Adam Jones's step-father." He shook Frank's hand. "Lieutenant Winters told me that you are the lead detective in the Seth Molloy case."

"Yes I am." He sat down and said, "What can I do for you?"

"I can't believe that you think Adam had anything to do with this. He's a good kid. He was just in the wrong place at the wrong time."

"I think it's awfully suspicious that he just happened to be at his long lost father's house that night. Did his mother tell him to do it?"

"Leave her out of it."

"I've been trying to track down your wife's whereabouts."

"You have? I don't know why you think she would be of much help."

"She was Molloy's ex-wife. She could tell me things about him. Where is she, Dr. Williams?"

"What difference does it make? You can't possibly think she had anything to do with her ex-husband's murder."

"Let's just say that I have a lot of unanswered questions where she is concerned. She has a lot of reason to want to see Seth Molloy dead. Where was she that night?"

"She was discharged from Pine Meadow that afternoon. We were driving to our summer home in Rehoboth Beach, Delaware."

Logan asked him for directions. Karl scribbled the address on a blank piece of paper and handed it to him. "She won't like it, but I guess there is no choice now."

"Finally," Logan said.

"She is emotionally fragile. I want to be there when you talk to her."

"All right," he promised.

Adam lay on his cot, staring out the small window. Only a hint of daylight cascaded into the cell. The metal bars on it created web-like shadows on the cement floor. He lost track of time. Studying the sun's position, he guessed it was early afternoon.

Waiting was the worst part. Maybe Detective Logan made a mistake. Maybe the judge would drop the case for lack of evidence like Donald Jenkins said. Adam could plead innocent all he wanted, but no one seemed to be listening.

All this alone time was not good for him. He always had to keep busy. He couldn't take time to think. His thoughts would inevitably revert to his childhood like an unwanted guest. He always wondered about the one big question that his mother never answered. She always changed the subject. Why did they change their names? Why didn't his father come looking for them? Why couldn't they return to their normal life? Why did she have to go to so much trouble to contact her family? Why wouldn't she let them see their grandparents? Why did she risk everything to keep them with her? Why did they always have to be on the move so much?

He knew the answers to all the questions, but dismissed them from his mind early on. He remembered watching, to his horror, the night that his father beat his mother up. Right in front of his own children. He started in on him—but Adam raced into his room and locked the door.

The screaming was horrifying. The sounds of furniture being tossed around the living room was frightening.

He knew at an early age that life wasn't fair. He was the man of the house at seven. He was always Yvonne's protector. He always had to protect their mother. He spent so much time in the protector role, that he never could have fun with kids his own age.

It took him the longest time to accept the fact that it wasn't his fault. None of it was. Opening up to women was difficult for him, until Maggie Albright came into his life when he was in college. She helped him so much. He never knew that happiness was possible until he met her.

He lay on the cot and stared at the bars separating freedom from life on the inside and outside. A guard whistled as he made his rounds. Other guards were engaged in lively chatter.

Adam concentrated on what was happening outside the cell, so he didn't think about Maggie.

He tried to convince himself that Logan was wrong and that he'd be sprung soon, but the more he thought about it, he just could not see a way out of this predicament. He wondered if Logan believed it when he told him he didn't remember what happened so long ago.

Karl stayed at Adam's apartment on the outskirts of town. The next morning, he went to the courthouse for the arraignment. He watched intently as the bailiff brought prisoners into the courtroom. Adam looked thin as a rail. His eyes were wide with fear. His hair was in his face. It looked like he hadn't slept in days. Adam exchanged a nervous look with his step-father, then sat on the front row.

Karl fought the urge to nod off, before Adam's case was called. About two hours later, Adam rose and pleaded not guilty. The judge set bail and called the next case. The bailiff took him back to his cell.

A guard rattled Adam's cell door and said, "Get up, you've been sprung!"

They went upstairs and Adam saw Karl waiting by the door. Adam threw his arms around him and said, "I thought you'd never get here."

Karl gave him the once-over and said, "You're thin as a rail! Haven't you been eating? Well, never mind that. We need to talk to your lawyer."

"Let's get something to eat first. I'm starving. They don't feed you much around here."

They headed out to the parking lot, when Logan approached them. Karl leaned over and whispered, "Just get in the car and don't say a word."

"Dr. Williams, I can help your step-son get a reduced sentence. But I need him to tell us who he was working with that night."

"He didn't break into the house, Detective."

"There are a lot of unanswered questions about his past that only he can answer."

"Not without my lawyer." He got in and slammed the car door. Then he sped down the road.

✳   ✳   ✳

CHAPTER 14

Thomas Smith glared at the framed Sears portrait of the Molloys over the fireplace mantel. They were all smiling and appeared to be a normal, happy family. But he knew otherwise. He could see it in Amelia's eyes that she was far from happy the day they posed for the photographer. Robby was three at the time. And Sarah was just a baby. Amelia was struggling to keep her in her arms.

Thomas wanted to take it off the mantel but Rose begged him not to. After she passed away, he didn't have nerve enough to remove it. He just let it remain the constant reminder of the pain that man caused to everyone involved. There wasn't a day that went by that he didn't wish the man was dead.

When his care giver went away for the day, he often puttered about his lonely rooms, asking God why a good woman like Rose was taken and a monster like Seth Molloy was allowed to live. If his hands weren't gnarled from arthritis, he would have killed the man years ago. At least his prayers were answered. The monster was hit on the head. He wondered why it couldn't have happened years earlier.

As he sat there watching the news, he tortured himself yet again. Could he have done more to help Amelia? Seth Molloy was a cunning adversary. He was so slick, he could steam-roll those who crossed his path with the flash of his amiable grin and the people wouldn't realize until moments later that he had done a number on them.

He remembered how sad Amelia looked during the custody hearing. She looked so old and tired. All the years of abuse contributed to her suffering. Seth looked suave and well put together in his pin-striped suit and feathered hair. He produced one document after another, further damaging Amelia's credibility.

"And here we have video footage of Amelia at a cocktail party," he had said. He pressed play and the images flashed on the small TV screen. "As you can see, it looks like she is tipsy. She can barely stand up. Guests have to help her stand up."

Footage shifted to another incident when the Molloys went out to dinner with the children. Wine glass in hand, Amelia stumbled across the room. When she came back, she practically fell on the table next to them as she tried to sit back down. Another scene depicted similar actions.

Seth pushed stop and the images faded to black. He addressed everyone present and said, "As you can see, your honor, this shows Amelia to be an unstable influence on our children. I am not the ogre that her attorney has painted me out to be. I am just a hard-working lawyer, trying to make a living for my family. If I work long hours, it is only to provide a roof over their heads and food to eat. I am concerned what happens when I am not at home. What would happen if she had a drink or two and something happened to the children? These issues need to be addressed, your honor. Thank you. I have nothing further."

Thomas remembered the look of horror in Rose's eyes. She looked pale. Tears formed in the corners of her eyes. He reached for her hand and it felt cold as ice.

"He is blowing everything out of proportion," she whispered.

Thomas was too stunned to answer her. He just sat there studying his son-in-law like a hunter observes his prey.

"We warned her, but she married him anyway," he said at last.

"Let's just pray that the judge awards custody to Amelia."

But that didn't happen. The day the judge announced the custody arrangement, it was as if time stood still. Thomas and Rose held each other's hands so tightly, they didn't even realize how much pain they were in. The pain in their hearts was bad enough. Amelia wailed uncontrollably. Thomas got up and held her in his arms. She was trembling.

"It would be in the best interest of the children if they were placed in the custody of their father, Seth Molloy," the judge said.

Amelia screamed, "No, you bastards! No!"

"Order in the court!" the judge cried. "I will have none of this in my court! If you can't contain yourself Mrs. Molloy, I will have a bailiff escort you out!"

"No, no, no, it's a travesty!" she shouted as bailiffs dragged her out. She struggled to pull free. "Don't you understand? He'll hurt them. He'll hurt them!" Her neck muscles strained. "You'll pay for this!"

Thomas and Rose watched helplessly as their daughter was escorted out. All he knew was that that monster was going to raise the children. He wouldn't blame Amelia if she plugged the man right there.

His legs felt rubbery as they exited the courtroom. They sat at a bench in the hall and waited until they were alone.

"Whatever you need, we're here for you, honey," he told her.

She closed her eyes and was quiet. After a long silence, she said, "He can't be responsible for the children."

Rose ran her fingers through her daughter's hair and said, "What do you want us to do, honey?"

"I don't know."

"Why don't you stay with us tonight?" Thomas suggested. "You shouldn't be alone right now."

Rose's words were warm and reassuring as they always were. "We'll get through this somehow."

They went back home, and Amelia took a long, hot shower to calm her nerves. Over hot chocolate, they thought of a plan...

Thomas regretted their decision to help Amelia escape with the children. None of them realized the gravity of the decision. It meant that they might never see her again. And they would never get to see their grandchildren grow up. As horrendous as that idea was, they knew that they did not have a choice. Seth would destroy them if he got custody.

He thought about the night they appeared at their doorstep to see them one last time. They begged her not to do it, but she wouldn't listen. They hugged their daughter and did not want to let go. He wiped tears from her eyes, like any good parent would do. Then they stood helplessly at the door, watching her carry a sleepy Sarah in her arms, while Robby tagged behind them. They watched the car pull out of the driveway and disappear from view around the bend. Then the lights faded in the night. He gripped Rose's hand and said, "Lord, watch out for them..."

Thomas leaned on his walker and slowly sat in his recliner. He cranked up the volume and continued watching the news until he fell asleep with the crossword puzzle on his lap.

* * *

CHAPTER 15

Yvonne gazed at the framed photo of Anthony on her desk. He looked so handsome in his uniform. He was the one person who gave her comfort when she was having a really rough day.

Working with battered and abused women on a daily basis took its toll on staffers. There was a high turnover rate. She definitely deserved a prize. She had almost made it to her second anniversary. She knew it was a depressing job, but she had it in her to help people.

She was much happier when she could lie in Anthony's protective arms in the safety of their bed. In the dark, he could not see the pain in her eyes. At this point, she didn't know if it was from work, or from her own personal nightmare from many years ago. When he was at sea, she tended to be a couch potato and ate too much.

Anthony gave her a sense of normalcy that she didn't have while growing up. She never felt like she belonged. Early childhood memories were foggy. At an early age, she was faced with fear and uncertainty. She never knew when they were going to be on the move again, where they were going, or when they would have enough to eat. She and Adam felt like prisoners. Their mother wouldn't let them go out and have fun. When they were walking down the street, their mother would cringe every time a cop walked by. They never went to parades, or any activities where they might see policemen. Yvonne learned to fear going out in public because of the way her mother reacted.

Her mother never stayed in any town long enough for Adam and Yvonne to make friends. Yvonne didn't want to get attached to kids her own age. She spent a lot of time alone studying in the library. She enjoyed reading and writing because of the escapism they offered. When she was junior high school age, she discovered painting. Her early artwork was disturbing, but vibrant, depicting her turbulent life on the run. Watching her mother self destruct added a frightening element to her artwork. Yvonne wished she could have helped her, but didn't know what to do. Never knowing why or what was happening was a scary thing for a girl at such a young age. School counselors detected a lot of anger and despair in her artwork and recommended that she talk to a therapist. Lynn ignored their suggestions. Yvonne kept the drawings in a private chest that had been moved from one town to another over the years.

When boys started showing interest in her, she acted cold and aloof. She declined going to parties, until classmates stopped inviting her. It didn't matter anyway, because her mother changed towns before Yvonne felt rejection.

Yvonne bottled up her feelings of confusion and anger where her mother was concerned. There were a lot of unanswered questions. She knew that something was wrong but couldn't put her finger on it. Every time she asked her mother questions, Lynn changed the subject. She was so secretive, it was like peeling onion layers to get information out of her.

Adam was old enough to remember about the events that led to their lives on the run, but couldn't talk about it.

The only thing Yvonne knew about Seth Molloy was from a few snapshots that she once found in her mother's bureau drawer. He was the perfect doting father with his baby girl on his lap. He was holding her in the air at the beach when she was two or three. Everybody was laughing. They looked happy. When she was about five, they all looked sad. Frightened was more like it. She always thought her father was dead. At least, that was what their mother told them when they were little kids. Adam knew it wasn't true but kept quiet about it.

Yvonne didn't realize her father was alive until she was much older and started figuring things out. Eventually, Lynn told her what really happened so long ago. Adam added his own, painful memories of being beaten up by their father. Fragmented childhood memories that Yvonne had blocked out, came flooding back.

The anger Yvonne felt toward Seth Molloy was palpable to this day. She often vowed that if she ever laid eyes on him again that she would get even for all the pain that he caused.

The telephone rang and she reached to answer it. "Hello?"

"Hi, hon."

"Hi, Karl. What's happening?"

He told her the latest information on Adam.

"I can't believe this is happening," she said. "Is there anything I can do?"

"Not really. Just sit tight and hope for the best, I guess."

"I feel so hopeless not being able to do anything about it."

"I'm afraid there really isn't anything you can do. I've got to talk to the lawyer. Detective Logan wants to talk to your mother."

"Why—why would he want to do that? There's nothing she could tell him that has anything to do with the case."

"That's what I tried to tell him, but he won't listen."

"I don't want that man to talk to her!" she was adamant.

"My hands are tied, hon. Well, I just wanted you to know what's going on. I'd better let you get back to work."

"I needed the distraction."

"Can you take a break? Your mom and I are at the beach. Can you come down for a couple of days?"

"That would be perfect. I'll see if somebody can switch with me."

"Good. We hope to see you there. Bye."

"Bye." She hung up and took a deep breath.

Her colleague Connie Stone popped her head in the door and said, "Gotta minute? We've got a woman that's an emotional wreck in Room five. Can you talk to her?"

"Sure." She got up and walked hurriedly out after Connie.

"It must be one of those days. Is there a full moon?"

"There must be," agreed Yvonne.

☆ ☆ ☆

CHAPTER 16

Maggie Albright met Adam Jones at college. Their relationship started out slow. He acted distant, but she didn't want to pry. As their friendship progressed, she became increasingly frustrated when he pulled away when they started to get closer. Whenever she asked him about his life, he was evasive and changed the subject. After a while, she had a long talk with Karl, who told her Adam had a lot of emotional problems and for her to just be patient. Adam slowly revealed himself like an onion peeling its layers. One night, he confessed that his real name was Robert Molloy. He told her about his mother's drinking problem. Eventually, he opened up and told her about his early childhood. He just told Maggie fragments from his memories.

She wanted to be intimate with him, but knew it was going to take a long time for him to get to that point. She didn't care. She was willing to wait for the man she was so desperately in love with. She knew that in time he would come around and they would finally have a chance for a fulfilling life together.

It was a major step in the right direction the day that Adam asked her to move in with him. The apartment wasn't much, but the surroundings didn't matter. They would move into a nicer place when they could afford it.

When she heard a car door slam, she went over to the window and peered out. She saw Karl walking toward the apartment building. A moment later, there was a knock at the door. She let him in and threw her arms around him.

"Oh, Karl. I'm so glad you could come."

"I'm just sorry it couldn't be under happier circumstances," he said.

Adam waved as he entered the living room.

"How are you making out?" Karl asked him.

He grimaced and said, "Not great. But at least I'm out of jail. Thanks for helping me out with it. I know it was a long drive and everything."

"I'd do anything for you and Yvonne."

Maggie went into the kitchen to get him a cup of coffee. Karl eased his way onto the sofa with the springs hanging out. Adam sat on a rickety chair across the room. Karl reached for the newspaper on the coffee table. He read a story that pertained to the Seth Molloy case, his eyes concentrating on a section about Adam.

Maggie came back in and handed Karl a mug. She looked at the newspaper article and scowled. "Isn't it awful?"

Karl nodded his agreement.

"What do you think?" Adam wondered.

Karl folded the paper and laid it on the coffee table. "Well, you admitted sending the death threats. That can't be good. But the police don't have enough evidence to convict you and they know it. You were just at the wrong place at the wrong time."

"It said in the paper that the police just found his blood on the doorknob and on the grounds," Maggie said.

"But they didn't find his blood anywhere in the house," Karl added. "Which means he couldn't have been in the house. The whole thing is ludicrous. The reason they didn't find anything is because he was never in the house."

"And if he wasn't in the house, that means he couldn't have killed the poor man."

"Exactly."

"That detective is persistent, though. I think he knows that his case is going nowhere."

"Do you think he'll try to sandbag Adam?"

"I don't know."

"Do you think he's an honest man?" Adam asked.

"He seems determined," Karl said. "If we can trust him, that's a whole different story."

A look of concern flashed in Maggie's eyes. "I wish this whole nightmare could be over so we could just get on with our lives."

"I know what you mean." Karl took a sip of coffee and placed the mug on the end table. "Lynn and I are going to the beach house. Why don't you both come along? It would really do you some good to get away for a few days."

Adam groaned and shook his head. "You know I can't leave town, Karl."

"I know. It was just a thought."

Adam looked at Maggie and said, "There's no reason you can't go, hon. I'll be fine here."

"I don't want to leave you here."

It didn't take much to make her change her mind. She told Karl she would try to get somebody to cover for her at work. About an hour later, Karl glanced at his wristwatch and said, "Oh, it's getting late. I need to get back to Lynn. It was really nice talking to you two."

Maggie grinned and said, "Thanks for stopping by. Have a safe trip."

"Thanks. I really do hope you can join us. The change of scenery would do wonders for us all. So long." He got up awkwardly and went out the door.

Adam turned the TV on loud and listened to the news while he chopped up a salad. She pulled out a vegetarian lasagna frozen dinner and popped it in the microwave. They didn't talk much during dinner. Afterward, they cleaned up in the kitchen. He watched the *Wheel of Fortune*, while she tidied up around the living room. Anything to keep her mind off the case.

Debbie Potter-Molloy felt like she was going to jump out of her skin. Detective Logan invaded her privacy with the ridiculous request to do the DNA swab. She wanted him to find out who killed her husband, not dredge up awful things about her personal life, as well. The very idea that he suspected her of killing her own husband.

The whole mess with the picture's in Seth's file cabinet was unsettling. Did Detective Logan accuse her of killing Seth over pictures of her and Raymond? She couldn't wrap her brain around it.

Then there was the matter of Raymond's gambling problem. She knew all about it, but had never called him on it, until now. She was in no mood for a confrontation today, of all days, but that was how it happened.

Raymond had just come back from a client's home, all dusty and dirty. She slammed the interior design catalogue shut and shot him a disapproving look.

"What's wrong?" he asked reluctantly.

"I can't believe you blew all our money at the tracks. What's wrong with you?"

"I'm sorry."

"Sorry doesn't cut it!" she screamed. "I'm trying not to lose my marbles over losing Seth and that detective practically accusing me of doing him in!"

"I promise, I'll make it up to you."

She waved her hand and shouted, "How? I've got Detective Logan accusing everybody I care about of doing such a horrible thing! And I've got you taking my hard earned funds out of the company's account, just so you can support your addiction to the horses!"

"I promise, I won't do it again."

"You're right. You won't do it again! Maybe–maybe I should get somebody else to work with me."

"Oh, Debbie. You can't do that. We've worked too hard to build up the business. Make it a success."

"Well, we won't have a business much longer if you keep it up!"

"You'll never find anybody as good as I am."

She pressed her fingers against her temples and took a few deep breaths to calm down. "I can't deal with this right now."

"I'll just go. Maybe–maybe we should talk about it later, when you're not so upset."

"That's a really good idea."

"We don't want to say things that we might not be able to take back." He patted her hand and said, "Maybe–maybe you should call it quits for the day. Go shopping. Try to relax. We'll–we'll talk about it later. Bye."

Her lips pursed. "Bye."

The bell jangled uncontrollably as he yanked open the door and slammed it. She watched him stomp past the shop.

✻　✻　✻

CHAPTER 17

As Logan headed south, he thought about how awful it must have been for the Molloy kids to have been raised by such a monster like Seth Molloy. His father was the total opposite of Seth Molloy, and Frank was glad about it. There was no emotional or physical abuse in the Logan household. Instead, Francis instilled discipline, love, and respect for others.

One of his happiest memories of Francis was on a beautiful summer day three months before he was shot. The Logans went on a picnic in the park. They spread out a blanket under the shade of a weeping willow tree, by the pond. Father and son spent the afternoon tossing a football to each other, while Mrs. Logan laid on the blanket, reading a romance novel.

If only Frank could have frozen that moment in time. It was the last time they got to do anything fun with each other. A few short weeks later, she became a widow when a drugged out dirt-bag gunned him down.

Logan sat in gridlock on Route 1, waiting to make a left toward Rehoboth Beach. He was shocked that there was so much

SECRETS CAN KILL

traffic on a weekday this early in May. It was such a nice day, kids and adults were probably playing hooky from school and work to sun worship. When the traffic light was yellow, he sped up to make it through the intersection. It turned red over his head. He glanced at the rear view mirror and grimaced at the line of motorists that didn't make it across in time. He shook his head and wondered why in the hell people thought it was so much fun going to the beach.

He looked to his left and right as he went over the bridge that led to the beach resort and admired the beautiful scenery. As he drove toward the boardwalk, he couldn't believe how many people were wandering up and down Rehoboth Avenue. It was so crowded, there were not many parking spots on the main strip. He turned onto a residential street and checked for the number. He pulled in front of an A-frame house that was nestled in the shade of pine trees, three blocks from the boardwalk. He got out and saw a twenty-something-year-old woman with long dark hair and sunglasses lying on a beach chair on the front porch. She looked familiar, but he didn't know where he had seen her before.

He walked up a brick walkway and smiled as he approached her.

"Good afternoon. I'm Detective Frank Logan from the Townsend Police Department in Pennsylvania. I'm looking for Lynn Williams."

"She isn't here. She's shopping until our attorney gets here."

"Do you know when he'll get here?"

"I don't know."

"Fine, then you won't mind if I sit here and wait? Maybe we could have a little chat."

143

Karl's voice boomed from the screen door: "Yvonne, don't say a word." He went outside to meet Logan. He had on a green short sleeve button-down shirt and brown shorts.

"I've had a long drive and I'm tired of playing these little games, Dr. Williams," Logan said.

"I'll tell you whatever you want to know, but leave them out of it," Karl said. "Let's take a walk."

They trekked up to the boardwalk and gazed at the ocean. Sun bathers lay strewn across the beach. Kids were frolicking with each other on the shore. Teenage boys clad in wet suits were surfing. Logan figured they went to school wearing bathing suits under their street clothes and cut their afternoon classes.

"Those boys are probably local kids," Karl said.

"I doubt much school work gets done this time of year."

"It is a nice day."

They walked up the beach and watched waves crash to shore. Seagulls squawked as they scoured the area.

"How long have you two been married?" Logan asked.

"About five years."

"How did you meet?"

"She was one of my patient's at the clinic I worked at in Arlington."

"Did she ever mention Seth Molloy?"

"Not at first." His attention focused on high school age kids playing catch with a Frisbee. They were laughing and having a wonderful time. "It took weeks for me to gain her trust. At first, she said he died. Every time I brought it up, she said she didn't want to talk about it so I didn't press her. I could tell she was scared or covering up something. She only told me bits and pieces. I think she was too frightened to tell me the whole story. I can't blame her.

Maybe she was afraid to tell me what her real name was. Maybe she figured it might slip out and Molloy would come after her."

They stopped and gazed at the ocean. Children darted by. Their shrill outbursts of laughter were unsettling to the ears.

Karl looked back at Logan and said, "As a doctor, I was trained not to get close to my patients. You should have seen the way she was when she was admitted. She came to us a broken shell of a woman. It's extremely difficult not to get emotionally involved."

"So as the weeks went by, you developed feelings for her?"

"Yes. I tried to suppress them, but I couldn't help but want to protect her. When she finally opened up to me, she told me all about her ex-husband."

"What did she say?"

"She talked about the custody battle."

"Was she afraid?"

"She was terrified. I don't know what kind of mental torture he inflicted on her, but it wrecked her. I blame Molloy for her drinking problem. She has spent the past fifteen years in and out of hospitals. She has been drinking on and off throughout our marriage. Her drinking problem practically destroyed our marriage!"

"You resented Molloy for that, didn't you?"

"Yes."

"You hated him so much, that you might have wanted to see him pay for what he did to her. Maybe you killed him or hired someone to do it."

"It's true, I hated the man. But I'm not foolish enough to kill."

"His death would have solved everything. You would have gotten your long awaited revenge."

"There are other ways to get even without resorting to murder."

"Have you ever had a fulfilling marriage with Lynn?"

"You're off base!" he snapped.

"You always played second fiddle to the memory of a long hated ex-husband. No matter how much she tried to repress her memories, she couldn't quite manage it. You were always second. You were her second husband. Your love was poisoned by memories of what he did to her. Am I close?"

"You're wrong!"

"You blamed him for making her live life on the run like an escaped criminal for years."

People walked by and Karl clammed up. When they had gone, they continued walking.

"That's true," Karl said after a long silence. "He dehumanized her! As her drinking problem worsened, she became more despondent...more bitter. And well, she was a different person. Not at all like the woman I married."

"I imagine that her hospital bills began piling up."

"I have insurance for her."

"Did you ever think about threatening Molloy and exposing him for the things he allegedly did?"

"The thought has passed my mind, once in a while," he admitted. "But what difference does it make now? If I had really wanted to do something like that, I would have done it a long time ago."

"Adam was at the house the night Molloy died. Maybe he killed him out of revenge."

"You don't know how to let up!" Karl stopped in his tracks and glared back at the detective.

"Or maybe you did it."

"You must be joking! We were driving down here that night."

"You never had a marriage to Lynn. You were always playing second fiddle to Molloy. No matter how kind you were to her,

Molloy's mistreatment of her always took over. Were you jealous? Maybe you wanted to get revenge."

"You don't know what it's like living in someone's shadow. Especially an ex-husband. I've changed my mind. She's suffered tremendously and I won't subject her to your grilling." He quickened his pace to lose the detective.

Logan hurried after him and shouted, "It's obvious that you really love her! You would do anything to rid her of this burden, wouldn't you?"

Karl ignored him and jogged down the beach.

When Logan went back to the house, Yvonne was still sitting on the porch. He tried to think of where he had seen her before. She looked familiar. Then he remembered the smiling woman he saw at the funeral. It was her.

They went inside and he looked around the living room. It had a definite beach theme about it. Wicker chairs were arranged in a semi circle around a coffee table. Water color paintings of beach scenes hung on the walls. She offered him tea and he accepted. Then she sat on a well-worn sofa in front of the window and looked uneasily at him.

"I need to ask you some questions, Sarah."

"My name is Yvonne," she corrected. "If you're going to ask questions, hurry up about it. This is a beach--a place to relax and escape problems."

"Do you remember anything about your father?"

"Very little," she admitted. "He used to take us places. Sometimes we went boating and fishing, but I don't really remember anything else. I was five the last time I saw him."

"Did your mother ever tell you why you were in hiding?"

She shook her head and said, "No. She told us one day that we were going to play a game and that I was to always be called Yvonne."

"Didn't you think that was odd?"

"You accept things when you're a child. You like to play games. When I got older, I realized there was something...not quite right."

"What do you mean?"

"I sensed that something wasn't right. She seemed...frightened...timid is more like it."

"Who or what was she scared of?"

"I don't know. She never said. She always told us that daddy was dead and we had to have new names. Then she started drinking." Her mouth quivered and her eyes moistened. Tears streaked her cheeks and she blotted them with her palms. "And then one night she was passed out on the floor. I was about ten. Adam and I panicked. He was about twelve and had so much responsibility put on him. He called an ambulance and...and we watched them take her out on a stretcher! They took her to the hospital, and that's where she met Karl. He was her therapist. He really helped her a lot. They fell in love and got married."

"What happened to you after she was taken to the hospital? Were you put in foster care?"

"She asked a neighbor to take us in for a few days. We couldn't take a chance on going to a foster family. We were scared that they'd check our records and find out our true identities."

"It must've been scary," Logan said softly.

She looked away. "Living on the run does something to you. It makes you not able to trust people."

"I'm so sorry you had to go through that. It wasn't your fault."

"It took me the longest time to realize that. A lot of therapy."

"Did she ever tell you that your father was alive?"

"When I was older."

"Did you ever try to contact him?"

"As I told you—I thought he was dead. I had no interest in meeting him. Knowing that he caused her so much grief, I didn't want to see him."

"When did you find out that he was alive?"

"I read a profile in a magazine. My mother was livid!"

"What did she do?"

"She broke down and cried. Locked herself in her room. I had to pry it out of her. It was an ugly scene."

He glanced at her wedding ring and asked, "What does your husband do?"

"He's a Navy SEAL. He's been at sea for six months and he'll be furious if he finds out that I was treated badly by a detective during an investigation. The same goes for the rest of my family."

"I'm trying to do my job, ma'am."

She removed her sunglasses and glared at him. "Let's put the cards on the table. I don't want my mother dragged through the mud. She's been through too much. I resent your lame accusations. What's the name of your supervisor?"

"Captain Ward."

"Well, if you give us any more trouble, I'll call him and talk about harassment. Then, you'll be out on the pavement."

He jotted: 'Yvonne is the hostile type' in his pad. Without listening, he continued his line of questioning. "You had some kind of agreement with your brother, didn't you?"

"What do you mean?"

"Did you agree to help him follow through with your mother's instructions?"

She looked blankly at him. "I don't know what you mean."

"Don't play dumb. Robert confessed to sending his father death threats to get his attention."

"His name is Adam!"

"He couldn't have done it alone."

She waved her hands and shouted, "You're out of line!"

"I know, but I have to ask these questions. Your father was also getting crank calls. Did you make them?"

"I don't know what you're talking about!" her voice shook.

"Where were you on the night he died?"

"I went shopping with a friend."

"Who?"

She folded her arms and huffed. "Adam's girlfriend."

"What's her name?"

"Maggie Albright," answered a woman who was standing in the doorway. She had on a tight fitting pink halter top and a short navy blue skirt. Strawberry blonde hair peaked out from under a red bandana.

"This is Detective Logan," Yvonne announced. Maggie stepped inside and went over to them.

"I know all about him," Maggie said sternly.

"May I have a word with you alone, Ms. Albright?"

"All right."

Yvonne went back onto the porch. She had had enough interrogation for one afternoon.

"Where did you go the night Seth Molloy was killed?"

"I went shopping with Yvonne."

"Where?"

"At the King of Prussia Mall."

"Did Rob's, I mean Adam's family ever mention Seth Molloy?"

"No, they kept quiet about it. I always thought something didn't seem quite right, but they never said anything. I'd ask some questions and they'd always change the subject or say it wasn't important."

"Do you love Adam?"

"Yes, he just asked me to marry him." She showed off her engagement ring.

"If he was out of work, where did he get the money to pay for a ring?"

"It belonged to his grandmother."

"So he did keep in contact with them."

"They worked out a secret code. A way he could call them—without Seth finding out."

"I get it. Three rings to let the person know you got home okay—and then don't pick up."

"Something like that."

He leaned forward and said, "I bet you would do just about anything for him, wouldn't you?"

"Of course I would." She regarded him skeptically. "What are you driving at Detective Logan?"

"He was out of work and in financial trouble, correct?"

"He was making out just fine doing odd jobs. And I work too. So we're not in too bad shape."

"Where do you work, Ms. Albright?"

"I'm a social worker in Norristown."

"Did he ever ask you to do things for him?"

She bristled and said, "I suppose so."

He reached in his jacket pocket and pulled out a photocopy of the death threat he found in Molloy's study. He waved it in her face and she gasped.

"He was receiving death threats, Ms. Albright. He was also getting crank calls. The person would call him and then hang up. And the same song played in the background every time. He got so spooked that he hired a private detective named Luke Springer to find out who was doing it. The person made the calls from different pay phones and Springer couldn't trace them before Molloy was killed."

"That's too bad."

"It is, isn't it? But everybody makes mistakes sooner or later. You can bet that I'll stay on it until I find out who made the calls."

"It sounds like a lot of work. I hope you find the sick bastard that did it."

"Adam admitted sending the death threats. Did you help him?"

"Of course not. How could you suggest such a thing?"

Karl marched into the room and glared at the detective. "Don't you dare accuse her of anything!"

"It's all right, Karl," she said calmly. "I'm fine."

He ran his hand through his salt- and-pepper hair. "It was a mistake for you to come here, Detective. When Lynn finds out—it'll upset her."

They heard a car pull into the driveway and Yvonne went to see who it was. She saw a heavyset man get out and walk toward the house.

Yvonne went to the front door and said, "I thought you'd never get here! I think I said things I shouldn't have said."

"We'll straighten it out." Donald followed her into the house and looked harshly at Logan. "You have so many holes in your case against my client, that I have no reason to doubt a jury will let him off on a technicality."

"We'll see," Logan said. He stared at Yvonne square in the eyes and asked, "What exactly did your father do to your mother?"

At that moment, they heard footsteps scraping along the ceiling. A door creaked and they heard thumping sounds down the steps. Logan saw a haggard looking woman come toward him with the aid of a cane.

"You wanted to see me, Detective Logan?" asked Lynn Williams.

✻   ✻   ✻

CHAPTER 18

"Yes, ma'am. You don't know how glad I am to meet you." She cleared her throat and everyone except Jenkins left the room. She sat facing the detective and said, "I knew it would come to this."

"Where were you on the night Seth Molloy died?"

"Karl and I were driving here straight from the hospital."

"Mrs. Williams, I know it's hard, but can you tell me what it was like living with Seth Molloy?"

She looked away and said, "He was a snake. I'm sure you've heard about what a wonderful man he was. Don't be fooled. People could be sucked in by his smooth talk and his powerful persona. He was a monster and I'm not sorry he's dead. I'm surprised it took somebody this long to kill him." She gazed out the window, deep in thought. She looked back at Logan and said, "Our marriage was on the rocks. It was only a matter of time. He was just starting out then. And I was standing in his way. He neglected me and I begged him for a divorce."

"Who filed the divorce papers first?"

"I did."

"How did he react?"

"He grew hostile."

"The custody hearing dragged on for weeks and the judge let him keep your children," Logan said. "You got so upset, that guards escorted you out of the courtroom. You were so terrified that he'd hurt the children that you were charged with kidnapping them."

"What choice did I have? He had a powerful temper when he had too much to drink. I didn't want him to hurt us anymore. He was a bastard. Very smooth. He destroyed all evidence that he—" She froze and looked away.

"Beat you," Logan said gently.

"Yeah, he beat me," she said without emotion.

"You don't have to say anything else," Jenkins advised.

"It's okay, I've got to do this." She met Logan's gaze and continued. "It was hell living with him. You don't know what it was like. Living in fear. He beat me so bad one time, I ended up in the hospital with cuts and bruises. He was drunk. I said I tripped. I made excuses. I didn't want to deal with him. He always said it wouldn't happen again, but one night he was furious and attacked me."

"Was this brought up in the custody hearing?"

"He made me look like a lush and convinced the judge that I was an unfit mother. I believe that's when my drinking problem really began. Living in fear of what he might do next...or if he'd do anything at all took its toll on me. It got to a point where I knew I had to get away from him. I didn't care at what cost.

"When he got custody of the children, I could have fought him. But I was worn out at that point. I knew what he'd do. What he was capable of. He'd make me out to be a lush...an unfit mother.

He'd cover his tracks. He'd win. He was the pillar of the community. I knew it was a lost cause."

"So that's why you took the children?"

She gripped the walker's rail, her voice trembling. "Yes! I couldn't live, knowing that he had his hands on them. It would have destroyed me."

"Were you afraid that he'd hurt the children?"

"Yes! I didn't want to take a chance, so I sneaked into the house that night...that's when I took them. I only told my parents about it...I remember, I drove off that night...terrified out of my head... but I was willing to do anything. I knew we didn't have any other choice but to start a new life in a far off town where no one knew us. I didn't know where I was headed...all I knew was that I had to get as far away from Seth as I could. Then, I heard about the kidnapping charges. We had to change our names. I lived in fear every day of my life that we'd be caught. Do you know what a fear like that does to your mental state?"

"No, ma'am," Logan said.

"It took its toll. I ended up in a hospital and my parents had to come take care of my children."

"Mrs. Williams, that is a mighty good reason to want Seth dead," Logan said as tactfully as possible.

"If I wanted Seth dead I would have killed him years ago! But then, I'd be in jail. My father would do anything for me, but asking him to change his name is asking too much. If he took care of the kids, Seth would have tracked them down. If I had killed him, I wouldn't have had to live the past twenty years in hiding. He would have been dead and the children would have been taken care of by my parents. Prison life would have been better than living on the run all this time. But I couldn't bring myself to kill him. I'm not capable of such a thing."

She buried her face in her hands and sobbed uncontrollably.

Logan gently patted her shoulder and said, "Thank you Mrs. Williams. I'm sorry that I upset you."

✻   ✻   ✻

CHAPTER 19

The name Amelia seemed foreign to Lynn Williams now. She laid back in her beach chair and watched waves crash to shore. She sipped iced tea and noticed happy young couples walk hand in hand with their small children. She smiled as she saw them disappear from view down the beach. That was what a happy family was supposed to look like.

She was glad Detective Logan left. Talking about what happened wasn't easy, but she felt better. Years of pain had eaten at her. He forced her to deal with it all over again. Painful memories came flooding back like unwanted guests. Her mind automatically flashed on that awful afternoon when Seth gained custody of the children. And then she thought about the night that she took off with them...

She went back to the house, two days after losing custody. She knew she had to get them out of there. Seth was taking a shower when she sneaked inside and went to Sarah's room. Her eyes lit up when she saw her mother come in.

"Mommy!"

Amelia leaned down and kissed her daughter's forehead. "Shh," she whispered as she took Sarah's hand. They slipped out and went to Robby's room down the hall.

Amelia turned the knob and popped her head in. When he heard the door open, he turned to see her come in. He leaped out of bed and ran into her arms.

"Mommy!"

She ran her hands through his tussled hair and kissed him on the head. "Come quickly," she whispered.

She held Sarah in her arms and then they walked hurriedly down the hall with Robby trailing along beside them. Amelia felt her chest heave as they descended the front steps. Her heart raced uncontrollably.

She didn't know what was worse, risking everything to get the kids away from Seth, or saying good-bye to her parents. A few minutes later, she arrived at their house, and mustered up the courage to see them one last time. She wiped away tears, and gathered Sarah up in her arms again.

A blast of cold air attacked Amelia's cheeks as she approached the house. Robby walked hurriedly alongside them.

The door opened and her parents looked dumbfounded at them. Amelia hugged her father and he wiped her tears gently with his fingers.

"Are you sure you want to do this?" he asked her.

"Yes."

"There are other ways."

"I don't care! I had to get them out of there."

"You'll be living in fear for the rest of your life."

"It's the chance I have to take."

"Think about what you're doing Amelia," her mother said. "Do you want to live like a thief on the run, for the rest of your life? You'll have to be in hiding at all times."

"We'll be okay." Her voice sounded shaky. She was trembling. She looked at her children and said, "From now on Robby, your name is going to be Adam. And Sarah--you're name will be... Yvonne. It'll be fun--like a game."

She looked back at her parents with apprehension in her eyes. "I'll write you a note to let you know where I am."

"Okay, then I'll destroy it," he said.

"Good. In another twenty-four hours, Amelia Molloy will cease to exist."

"Take care of yourself." He held her in his arms and tried to stop her shaking, like any good father would do. But he couldn't help her. He closed his eyes and bit his bottom lip so he wouldn't cry.

Her eyes welled with tears. "You too. Take care of yourself. I love you."

She buried her head in her mother's arms and never wanted to let go.

"There are other ways. You don't have to do this. We can fight for custody."

"We've been through enough already, Mom," Amelia said. "I've made my mind up." She kissed her mother's cheek and slowly pulled away. "Thanks for all your help. I love you."

"Please don't do this!" she implored. "The children need a stable home life. Think about what this is going to do to them."

"I don't care! I need to do what has to be done. We can still see each other...but it won't be so easy. I'll be in touch." She hugged her again and was on her way.

She carried a sleepy Sarah in her arms, while Robby tagged behind them. Robby climbed on the back seat, and Amelia laid Sarah next to him. She put a blanket over them and slammed the door. She slipped behind the steering wheel. Then she wept uncontrollably as she waved to her parents one last time, and pulled out of the driveway.

Her thoughts drifted to her life on the run. She hated all the secrecy. Forcing her children to lie was the worst part. Living on the run under the assumed names of Jones caused them years of emotional turmoil. They could never settle down. They could never make friends. They were always living in one town after another... one big lie.

She thought about the danger she put the kids through. The fear that they would get caught. And then she thought about the one woman who she could talk to at a diner in a forgettable town in the midwest...

Lynn leaned down and stacked dirty plates, one on top of the other, and hoisted them over her head as she headed toward the kitchen. This week she sported a red hairdo. When she wasn't at work, it stretched to her shoulders. At work, it was tied neatly under a hair net.

The older couple with their screaming grandson at table seven was quickly replaced by eight truckers. They ranged in age from twenty-something to mature adults. If you could call them mature. They were young at heart and fit in well with their younger counterparts.

They came in once a week. She had totally lost track of time. Was it Wednesday already?

She didn't have to memorize what they would be ordering. They usually ordered the same thing. Ron liked eggs over easy and a lot of bacon. He had kind eyes, so she usually stuck in an extra one. Duke was a T-bone steak man. Jimmy liked cheeseburgers with a lot of cheese and fries. The others liked to eat and drink heartily.

She leaned in on Duke and winked. "What'll it be, honey?"

His eyes twinkled. "The usual, baby," he answered sweetly.

"Want coffee with that?"

He held out his mug and said, "Go for it."

She poured him another cup of coffee. The others held out their cups and she repeated the ritual.

She slipped into the kitchen to place the order and came back to wait on a group of smartly dressed men and women at the table next to them.

Banker Lyle Coventry grinned at her and said, "How are the kids, Lynn?"

She smiled and said, "Oh, they're doin' just fine. Thanks for asking."

She took their drink orders and disappeared into the confines of the kitchen. By the time she took their orders, she was ready for a smoke break.

Thankfully, the lunch rush thinned out about one thirty. She went out back with fellow waitress Anna Dumphries and leaned against the building. They lit up and blew smoke skyward.

Anna took one look at her and said, "Rough day?"

"Rough year." She took a deep drag and slowly exhaled.

"And we're only half way through our shift."

Lynn closed her eyes and drew a deep breath. "Don't remind me."

"Wouldn't it be nice to just quit and take a cruise 'round the world?"

"It would be nice. But who could afford it?"

"Really."

"I can barely get by as it is."

"I know what you mean," Anna agreed.

"I might have to take a second job. Or work longer hours."

"Know what you should do? Marry a rich guy."

"Been married. Don't need that hangup again."

"You just haven't found the right guy."

"I don't think there are any of them out there."

"They're there. You just ain't lookin' hard enough."

They stubbed out their cigarettes and went back inside. By four o'clock, Lynn felt totally drained. She did not think she had the strength to last another four hours. Fortunately, it was the slow time. There were only a handful of customers.

The wait staff had to work overtime. Rita had the flu, and Cindy just gave birth to a ten pound baby boy. Lynn didn't think she would be able to handle another long shift. She couldn't wait until Rita and Cindy came back.

Lynn and Anna took this momentary slow time to sit and have coffee and salads. By now, Lynn's feet ached from standing on them all day. A ten minute break would do wonders.

"My folks are comin' for the holidays," Anna reported. "What 'bout you? Are your folks comin' for Thanksgiving?"

Lynn met her gaze and smiled shyly. "Oh, I'm afraid they can't make it. They're comin' from so far away—the traffic is just awful."

"I know. We hate the crowds." She poured creamer in her mug and stirred heartily. She looked back up at her and said, "You never did tell me where they're comin' from."

"I didn't? Sorry."

Anna leaned forward and said, "What's the big secret? We all gotta come from somewhere, don't we? Unless you was beamed down here or somethin' like that."

Lynn yawned and closed her eyes. "Sometimes I feel like I'm from another planet by the end of the day."

"Tell me about it." Anna took a sip of coffee and looked intently into Lynn's blue eyes. "Where are they from?"

"Back east."

"Which state?"

"Are you a cop?"

"No, silly."

"They're from Virginia."

Anna tapped her hand. "There, that wasn't so hard. God, Lynn, sometimes I worry about you."

"You don't need to."

Their solitude was interrupted when hostess Shelley Murphy went over to inform them that she had just seated a couple at table four.

"That's me," Anna said as she got to her feet. "Ta-ta."

Lynn took her cue and helped set up tables in her area. An hour before her shift was over, two State Patrol officers entered the room. Her stomach felt like it was going to knot up when she laid eyes on them. It was the same feeling she always got when she saw law enforcement officers. She studied their faces to see if she knew them. One was tall and blond, about thirty. The other was shorter, with brown hair and a dark complexion. He was about the same age.

Her eyes darted around her section. Thankfully, her tables had hungry customers. She looked back at them and their eyes met. The blond silently sized her up with a subtle smile and look. They sat at the counter and hid their faces behind menus.

Every time she went into the kitchen, she avoided looking at them. But she didn't want to be obvious, so she occasionally gave them a warm smile.

Living life on the run was a bear. She hated the secrecy. She especially could not stand knowing the pain and confusion she was causing her children. They didn't understand. And she couldn't explain what was happening. Maybe when they were older. Maybe then they would understand. Until then, it was a waiting game... one of these days someone would recognize her. She lived in fear of someone recognizing her. Tonight, these cops didn't notice her. But what about the next ones that came in?

She was only so glad to clock out. She got in her beat up station wagon and lit a cigarette. She drove through town and pulled into their trailer park. She looked both ways before going inside. The place wasn't much, but it offered warmth and security. Little Adam was on his knees doing his homework at the coffee table. Yvonne was at the kitchen table, hovering over her Grammar lessons. The TV was on in the background and offered a cheerful comedy in their otherwise humorless lives at the moment.

She told them about the cops at the diner, and nothing else. They told her about their days.

When Adam told her some kids asked if he could go play ball with them on Saturday afternoon, she gave her standard response of "Are you kidding?"

Adam folded his arms and shot her an evil look. "Why not?"

"Somebody might recognize you, sweetie."

"That isn't fair!" he snapped. "Nobody knows who we are in this stick town!"

"You never know."

He got up and marched to his bedroom. He slammed the door and shouted, "It isn't fair!"

Yvonne lifted her head from what she was doing and asked, "Why won't you ever let us play with our friends, Mommy?"

Lynn went over and put her arms around her little girl. "Because it's complicated."

"Why is it complicated?"

"There are bad people out there that want to hurt us, sweetie."

She looked at her wide-eyed. "You're scaring me, Mommy."

Lynn squeezed her gently and closed her eyes. "I don't mean to, sugar. It's just the way it's gotta be right now. I did something I shouldn't have done—and they'll put me in jail if they know we're here."

"What did you do?"

"I can't explain right now. Just do as I say—for now."

"Then can we go play with our friends?"

"Maybe later." She hustled about in the minuscule kitchenette and nuked three microwave dinners. They sat in awkward silence at the small round kitchen table. Adam glared at her, using his icy silence to get back at her. Yvonne didn't know quite what to say, so she said nothing. Lynn tried to ease the tension by talking about her hectic day. Adam finished eating and shoved his dirty plate in the sink. Then he locked himself in his room all night. When his favorite TV show came on, Lynn knocked on the door to let him know. He was too busy and didn't come out.

Lynn sat on the sagging sofa and watched alone, while Yvonne colored at the kitchen table. Tears welled in Lynn's eyes, for she knew what their sacrifice was costing the kid's relationships.

She knew she had no other choice. The children were having to sacrifice so much if they could not meet new friends. She really felt bad about it but what else was she supposed to do?

She went to bed at eleven and watched the local news till she fell asleep. She awoke at six o'clock to start the whole ritual over again...

A screaming child jarred Lynn back to reality. She felt tears moisten her cheeks, and adjusted her sunglasses. The beach was no place for a crying woman. She gathered her beach paraphernalia and marched toward the boardwalk.

☆   ☆   ☆

CHAPTER 20

When Logan got to the station on Monday morning, it was one of those days when nothing went right. He was disappointed to learn that the scratches on Seth Molloy's chest did not come from Debbie Molloy. The DNA results did not match. It was back to square one. The samples taken from Seth's fingernails indicated that he did not scratch his assailant, so they would have to find other avenues to determine the killer's identity. Late that afternoon, he went back to Debbie's house with Jim Anderson and told her the good news.

"It was a waste of time," she said. "I told you so."

"It had to be done," Logan informed her. "You admitted getting into a nasty argument with him prior to his murder. And there was a scratch on his chest. I'm going to need to collect swabs from Raymond and the kids."

She had a few choice words for them, but restrained herself from using foul language for the younger children's sake. After major complaints from the boys, Jim collected their swabs and said, "There, that wasn't so bad. I'm sorry we inconvenienced you all. Have a nice day."

"I don't know what you hope to gain by doing this," Raymond said. "The killer will get away Scot free and you'll wind up with nothing from us."

"We are actively pursuing other suspects, sir," Logan assured him. He followed Jim out without saying another word.

Raymond gritted his teeth and said, "Can you believe the nerve of those guys?"

Passersby walk hurriedly down the street. The building looms in the foreground. A man pops out of the front door and waves the people in. Images of the grand entryway move in slow motion. He smiles, and people pile onto the elevator. It takes forever to reach its destination. The door opens and it is another slow pan of the obnoxiously red carpeted hall. All of a sudden, a door appears out of nowhere. It is the same door that he sees all the time. Then there is a gun shot...

Frank awoke with a start and wiped perspiration from his face. That recurring dream kept him from drifting back to sleep. The digital clock on his bedside table read four thirty a.m. Every time he drove past that building, his thoughts automatically drifted to that awful afternoon. His subconscious could not escape it.

He could not get the case out of his mind. Debbie Potter-Molloy had the perfect motive. Seth had compromising pictures of her and Raymond Sinclair. She was afraid she would lose custody of the kids if those photos surfaced during the divorce proceedings. Unfortunately, her DNA did not match the scratches on Seth's chest, so that meant that she could not have injured him during the struggle the night he was murdered.

He worried that Adam Jones would get off on a technicality. His DNA swab also did not match the scratch on Seth's chest. His fingerprints were on the doorknob, and his blood splotches were on the grounds leading to the front curb, which placed him at the scene of the crime. Unfortunately, there was no physical evidence that he had been in the house. He admitted sending the death threats, which was a felony. That should count against him, but he had no idea what Donald Jenkins would do to get his client off.

No prints were on the poker used to hit Seth on the head, which meant that the killer used gloves. He couldn't get Jones to reveal the identity of his partner, and he had no leads.

Right now, Raymond Sinclair seemed to be the most likely suspect. He lost money at the race tracks. With Seth Molloy dead, his grieving widow stood to get a lot of money from his life insurance policy. It would be enough money to pay back his gambling debt, if Sinclair married her. It was the perfect motive for wanting to bump off Seth.

He wondered if Jones and Sinclair were in on it together. The only way he would find that out, was to bump up his surveillance on Raymond. Then he would concentrate on Adam.

Logan tossed and turned in bed, but nothing seemed to work. He just couldn't sleep. Finally, he turned on the light and reached for a spy novel on the bedside table.

☆　☆　☆

CHAPTER 21

It was Frank's turn to party in Penny's world on Friday, May 9th. There wasn't anything he detested more than having to get all dressed up for than the fancy office party shindigs that she dragged him to. He was just thankful that it didn't happen on a regular basis. Even still, her colleagues were stiffs in suits and ties. There wasn't enough alcohol to loosen him up around them. They spoke of things he didn't understand. When financial topics were brought up, his eyes glossed over. He knew he had to make an effort for her sake.

The party was held in the ball room at the Marriott. Her colleagues mingled over cocktails. The only positive thing about the evening was Penny. She looked stunning in a burgundy evening dress that matched the highlights of her hair. She introduced him to her coworkers and he forced himself to make small talk. He was used to dealing with interrogating suspects, not corporate types. Unless they were charged with embezzlement or murdering their spouses, he had a hard time talking to them.

The Senior Vice President of the bank cornered him at the bar. He was about sixty, with heavy jowls and short white hair. Wire-rimmed glasses hung over a beak-like nose. Frank smiled to be polite. It was a forced smile. The man in the tailored suit did all the talking. Did Frank want to increase his portfolio? Did Frank know that if he transferred funds into various accounts that he would improve his financial status?

Penny sidled up next to them, all smiles. She linked her arm in Frank's and said, "Oh, I'm so glad you two had a chance to meet."

"It's nice to know how the other half lives," Logan said with a hint of sarcasm.

"And I get to hang out with his buddies from the police station," she said.

Henry Brown smiled and said, "You must meet a lot of interesting people in your line of work."

"Some people are good, and some aren't so much."

"I understand you are working on the Seth Molloy case. How is it going? Do you have any leads?"

"Not that I can discuss right now. Sorry."

"The custody case was big news back in the day. It was such a tragic story. His ex-wife must have been frantic, to have done a thing like that."

"I can't imagine what it must have been like," agreed Logan. He asked the bartender for another glass of Merlot and politely excused himself.

About an hour later, only a few guests remained. Penny whisked Frank outside, and they marched down the sidewalk. She was eerily quiet, and Frank sensed that she was in one of her moods again.

"I did the best I could," he said. "You know I'm not good at this sort of thing."

"I hang out with your friends. And sometimes it isn't easy. You guys are too–clickish."

"I'm sorry."

"It's not that I don't like your friends, but sometimes I feel like an outsider."

"You seemed to hit it off well with Harry's wife."

"She's a lot of fun," agreed Penny. "But sometimes I think you could try a little harder to fit in with my friends."

"It's hard for me. We don't speak the same language."

"I get that. But it's starting to tick me off a little bit."

He waved his hands up in the air in protest. "Come on. I don't want to spend what little time we've got together in a big fight."

"Okay, fine. We'll discuss it later."

Later never came. It was something that was bubbling under the surface. She accepted the fact that Frank spent too much time at work. She agreed that he needed to work extra hard to make sure a criminal didn't go free. But they had reached a crossroads in their relationship. He needed to have a life outside the police station. So far, their only free time together centered around his coworkers. Unfortunately, a compromise did not seem to be in the works.

✼　✼　✼

CHAPTER 22

Logan knew that Penny was peeved. She hadn't returned his calls for three days. By Monday, he wondered if she would ever speak to him again. He did what he always did after one of their tiffs. He concentrated his efforts on solving the Seth Molloy case. He didn't know which was worse, worrying about a case that wasn't going anywhere, or wondering how he could make Penny realize that she had to take him as he was. He decided to give her some space. He would let her get in touch with him when she cooled off.

About a month later, he knew something wasn't right when he called to invite her to go to the beach with him for Memorial weekend. Instead of spending the weekend with the woman he loved, he listened to Flosky jabbering the whole way there and back. Every woman that Joe met at the beach could be the next Mrs. Flosky. He impressed them with his lack-luster charm, bragging about fighting crime.

Returning to work on Tuesday morning was an adjustment at first, but it didn't take long to get back into the swing of things. There were no new leads in the Molloy case, so they waited for another case to come their way. To kill some time, they played catch with a Nerf ball that Joe kept in his desk drawer.

Logan got back to his apartment about ten p.m. and leaned down to pick up a pile of mail. It was mostly bills and the usual junk mail. He plopped on his sofa and turned on the TV. His face brightened when he saw Penny's handwriting. He tore open the letter and read it. But it wasn't pleasant news.

"Dear Frank,

This is the hardest thing I've ever had to do. Don't take it personally. You know I love you and wouldn't want to hurt you.

I think we should stop seeing each other. I know you love your job and I wouldn't want you to give that up. Sometimes I think you spend too much time trying to crack a case, and not enough time away from the office. I understand that you have to work hard so the bad guy doesn't go free. I've always had fun hanging out with the gang at Barney's, but I don't think you've ever really tried hard enough to fit in with my friends from work. We keep coming back to this problem and I don't see a way around it. I don't think you'll ever change.

Remember the good times we shared. I'm sorry.

Love Penny."

He wadded up the letter and threw it across the room. "Damnit!"

Logan worked over time for the next few days to keep his mind off the break up. He just wanted to get the damned Molloy case solved.

"Do you want to talk about it?" Joe asked.

"No," he grumbled.

"I know you're upset, but don't take it out on us. I'm just telling you as a friend to lighten up. We've all been there."

"I'm sorry if I've been grouchy lately. I'll keep my thoughts to myself." He looked back at the pile and buried himself in work. The phone records he got from private detective Luke Springer were not getting him anywhere.

"Do you need any help?"

"No!" Logan snapped. He tapped his pen and reviewed his notes until frustration set in. Nothing was coming to him. He handed Joe half of the pile of phone records. "Here, maybe you'll see something I missed."

Flosky's jaw dropped when he saw the endless lists of telephone numbers. "This could take hours."

Logan groaned. "Tell me about it."

A few minutes later, Joe looked up from the pile and asked, "You've been following Raymond Sinclair some more. Have you found out anything new about him?"

"Not really."

"Right now, he seems to be our number one suspect, wouldn't you say?"

"It looks that way," he said without looking up from the list.

Frank didn't think things could get any worse, until Harry Winters went over to them and said, "I hate to rain on your parade, Frank, but Sinclair came in while you guys were out and told me he went to a mini-mart near Molloy's house on the night he was murdered. He said it slipped his mind with all that was happening. I went to talk to an employee there and he said Sinclair came in about quarter of eight. He was on the video surveillance camera with the time and date on it."

"Oh great!" Logan cried. "Now what?"

"I guess that rules him out as a suspect," Harry said.

Logan pounded the desk and swore. "I guess I'll have to keep tailing Adam Jones."

"Maybe you'll catch him talking to his partner," Harry said on his way out.

"I don't believe it!" Logan exclaimed.

"Don't worry, Frank. Something's bound to come up," encouraged Joe. "It always does. Sinclair still had time that he could've gotten over to Molloy's home. Maybe Adam Jones ran out of the house later than when Mrs. van Horn thought he did."

He contemplated it a moment and said, "That's possible."

"We'll figure this out, Frank."

Logan let out a deep breath and concentrated on the telephone list. "It's like looking for a needle in a haystack. Maybe if we're lucky, we might just find what we're looking for before the turn of the century."

"That'll be a long time from now, Frank. I'm sure we'll both be dead then."

"What are we overlooking?" He tapped his pencil and flipped the page.

Joe looked over at him and said, "Come on, Frank. You need to take a break. You've been working yourself silly on the case. Nothing that a Friday night out at Barney's won't fix."

"I know what you're trying to do and it won't work."

"Come on, you need to take your mind off things. Have some fun."

"Not tonight. You guys go without me."

Joe persisted until Frank gave in. "All right, I'll go for a little while."

"Good. Maybe if you go, you won't be so cranky."

About six o'clock, Logan called it a day and got a cheese steak at the deli down the street.

Frank didn't know why he let Joe talk him into going to Barney's on Friday night. After getting Penny's letter, he didn't feel like being around anybody at the moment. He preferred puttering around the apartment, feeling sorry for himself. He just wasn't in the mood to hang out with his buddies. He pretended to be cheerful.

Joe slapped his shoulder and said, "Come on, Frank. You gotta lighten up. It ain't the end of the world. Maybe she'll change her mind."

"I don't think so this time." He finished off his Coors light and poured another mugful. "We've got issues."

Harry chuckled and said, "Who doesn't?"

Megan gripped his hand and laughed. "It took him the longest time to be litter trained!"

"It's hard as hell sticking my butt against that stuff," Harry said. "But I got used to it. Her biggest issue is the classic toilet seat lid up or down problem that has plagued couples for a hundred years or so," Harry said.

"How old is the toilet anyway?" Joe pondered.

"I wonder if couples ever had these problems with outhouses," Harry added. "If so, the problem must go back even further than that."

"Well, at least you pick up after yourself now, Harry," she said. She looked at the others and said, "It took him the longest time to clean up after himself."

"And it took a lot of my patience to learn to wait for you to fix yourself up."

She ran a hand through her red hair and said, "Well it's worth it, isn't it?"

He leaned forward and kissed her. "You don't need much time fixing yourself up. You're perfect as is."

"You say the sweetest things!" She leaned in and returned for another kiss.

Frank groaned and said, "Get a room!"

Joe laughed so hard that he almost choked on his chips. "Can't you guys see that we're trying to eat here?"

They all laughed. Harry finished off his beer and poured another mugful.

Joe glanced around the room and said, "I don't see Jenna here tonight. She said she'd be here."

"Is she the new love of your life, Joe?" asked Frank.

"Maybe," he said with a wry smile.

"I thought Mary was the woman you were going to marry," Harry said.

"I guess it just wasn't in the cards. Now Jenna has real potential."

Frank's right eyebrow arched. "And you know this how?"

"I just got a feeling."

Frank smiled behind his beer as he listened to Joe talk about the new woman in his life. Anything to keep his mind off the break up. Eventually, the subject reverted back to Penny.

Harry took a swig of his beer and said, "You could try a little harder to fit into her world, Franky."

"Now you're sounding like my grandfather."

"She hangs out with us all the time. I don't blame her for bein' mad that you don't want to associate with her coworkers. It's just a thought."

"I'm no good in those situations," Frank said with a wave of the hand. "I realize I've got a problem in that department."

"Rudimentary social skills, you mean?" chided Harry.

"Gimme a break, Winters. You know how it is. I prefer hanging out with you guys."

"Because you feel more comfortable around the guys," Megan continued. She wasn't a cop, but she could be as hard-nosed as Frank was when he was interrogating a suspect. "You need to try to do what she wants a little bit. Maybe if you do she'll want you back."

He took a healthy swig of his beer and thought it over. "I'll think about it."

"I hope you do. 'Cause we can't stand a gloomy Gus around here."

When a Kenny Chesney song blasted in the background, she tapped Harry's hand and practically yanked him off his feet. They scrambled over to the tiny dance floor and bounced around to the music. They were having a grand old time.

Frank laughed as he watched them strut their stuff. A few weeks ago, he and Penny had fun like that.

Joe looked over at him and said, "Why don't you give her a call?"

"And say what?"

"Why don't you go to Philly and take a quiet walk in the park or something? You don't have to talk about anything. Just relax and have a good time."

Frank took another swig and nodded. He glanced at the clock behind the bar. It was half past twelve. He finished off his beer and said, "I'm beat. I'm gonna head on out."

"Party pooper!" Joe cried. "Come on, at least stay till last call."

Frank grinned and said, "I'll see you later." He got up and pushed through the crowd.

☆   ☆   ☆

CHAPTER 23

Logan awoke at four thirty a.m. Saturday and put on a flannel shirt and blue jeans. He poured coffee into a large metal canteen, and gathered his fishing gear. He packed the car, and pulled onto the lonely dark road. As he drove toward the Jenkintown retirement community, he thought about his grandfather. A year ago, Gramps underwent hip replacement surgery and convalesced at a nursing home outside of Townsend. After an aggressive two month rehabilitation regimen he was able to get around with the aid of a cane now. Frank helped him move into an apartment at Frenchtown, and tried to visit him as often as his schedule allowed. He fought back an incredible feeling of guilt that he didn't visit him as much as he should.

Gramps was the one constant in Frank's life. But it wasn't always that way. After Frank lost his parents at such an early age, Gramps took him in. Their relationship was challenging, to say the least. Gramps had just lost his wife, Helen, and also was grieving. The obedient and kindhearted Frank turned into an unrecognizable moody teenager. He was a gangly, long haired fourteen-year-old.

Despite his efforts, Gramps felt that he was failing badly. Franky spent his free time in his room. He stopped playing football with his friends. He was miserable and took it out on Gramps.

One day, Gramps was having a disaster in the kitchen. He got distracted by a telephone call, and burned dinner. He dared to knock on Franky's bedroom door. The music was so loud, he couldn't hear him.

"Franky. Yoah, Franky." He knocked a little bit harder. "Franky! Are you okay?"

The music wasn't as loud. Gramps heard Franky's loud footsteps pound toward the door. The door opened a crack and he peered out, oily complexion and all.

"What do you want?" he snapped.

"A friend got me on the phone and I burned dinner. So, why don't we go down to Vinny's and get pizza?"

"I'm busy! Just order something."

Gramps smiled like he always did and said, "All right. I can see that you're busy. I'll call you when it's ready."

Franky slammed the door and turned the volume back up. The music was blaring. Gramps felt like he was about to jump out of his skin. It was so bad, he couldn't even make out what the singers were saying.

When the pizza was delivered, he went back up to tell him it was ready. Franky was nastier than before.

"I'm busy!"

"It'll get cold."

"I don't care! I'll warm it up! That's what microwaves are for!"

"All right. I don't want to bother you."

He went back downstairs and sat at the table alone. The music jarred his concentration. About an hour later, Franky shuffled into the living room while Gramps was watching the news.

"Where's dinner?" he demanded.

Gramps smiled and said, "I put it in the fridge."

Franky marched into the kitchen and yanked open the refrigerator door so hard that it hit the counter.

"Hey, be careful with that!" Gramps yelled back.

But Franky didn't apologize. He ripped off three pizza slices and flopped them on a plate. He nuked them and sat at the kitchen table. He stuffed large chunks into his mouth and chewed them with such a vengeance that Gramps didn't recognize his own grandson when he went into the kitchen to get a glass of water.

Franky didn't even acknowledge that his grandfather was even in the room. Gramps sat facing him and just gaped at him in disbelief.

"What's wrong with you?"

"Nothing."

"Don't give me the nothing line again. You've been moping about the house for weeks and I want to know why. I don't deserve to be treated this way. I'm only trying to help you, and you aren't giving me one ounce of appreciation. I know you're upset. You lost your parents. Well, I just lost my wife, too. You don't see me moping about, angry at the world!"

Franky picked up his plate and glass and stomped over to the door. "Leave me alone! I don't want to talk about it!"

He started to head for the steps, when Gramps yelled, "Come on, Franky. Why don't you watch TV with me? It doesn't have to be the news."

He glared back at him and shouted, "I said I'm busy!"

Gramps started in on him, but he was already upstairs. He slammed the door so loud, Gramps felt the vibration in the hall. Two hours later, Franky plopped next to him in the living room, a totally different boy. Gramps looked at him incredulously a moment, wondering how that unruly brat could have been transformed into Prince Charming in such a short time period.

"What are you watching?" Franky chirped.

"A James Bond movie."

"Oh."

When a commercial came on, Gramps looked sharply at him and said, "We need to talk about the way you acted at dinner, young man."

"I'm sorry." He pushed hair out of his eyes and focused his attention on the activity on the TV screen.

"You have been acting like this for weeks and it is going to stop now. I can't take much more of your mood changes. I know you're upset. So am I."

"It isn't fair."

"Who said life was fair? We're both grieving. We're going to have to learn to work together. I know it's not easy, but you're going to have to try to cooperate with me. How do you think your mom and dad would feel if they saw you treating me like this?"

He stared blankly at him and said, "They wouldn't like it."

"Good. Now we're getting somewhere. You need to honor their memories. To do that, you need to be on your good behavior. Treat people the way you would want to be treated. Got it?"

"I guess so."

"No guessing, mister. From now on, I want you to treat me with respect. No more gloomy Gus. Got it?"

Franky twirled his hair and said, "Whatever."

"Sometimes I feel like I'm in over my head. I haven't raised a kid your age in a very long time. Since I don't know what I'm doing, maybe–maybe we should talk to a grievance counselor. I don't pretend to have all the answers. Maybe a counselor would know the right things to say."

Franky sat up straight and shot him a look. "I don't need to talk to a shrink!"

"Yes you do. You aren't acting right. Come on, if you do it, I'll try to fix whatever it is that you think I'm doing wrong."

"You aren't doing anything wrong. You've been great." Tears welled in his eyes. "I just wish things could go back to the way they were."

He sat next to him and rubbed his arm. "You know that can never be. You're stuck with me." Franky burst into tears and Gramps cradled him in his arms. They sat there rocking each other.

"It isn't fair!"

"I know," Gramps said gently. "We'll get through this. I promise."

Gramps kept to his promise. After a few therapy sessions, Franky worked out his anger problems and developed into the kind of man that his parents would be proud of. The journey there was painful, but forged an everlasting bond between the older man and his grandson.

Frank pulled into the parking lot and went inside. A woman at the reception desk looked up and smiled at him. The halls were vacant at this early hour. He wound his way to his grandfather's room and knocked on the door. Gramps was all dressed and ready to go. He took one look at his grandson and said, "Is that a caterpillar on your lips?"

"Very funny. It makes me look older and more distinguished."

"It makes you look like a little kid with dirt on his face," he said laughing.

"I had to do something."

"Why?"

"People say I look like a kid."

"Be happy that you have a youthful appearance. Some day, when you're old like me, you'll be glad."

"You aren't old Gramps. And you look ten years younger."

Gramps smiled and said, "I know."

They went out to the parking lot and Frank packed his grandfather's gear in back of his car. He slammed the trunk and climbed behind the driver's seat. Then he pulled down a windy country road that led to their favorite spot to fish.

They sat down at the end of a small dock and cast out their lines. At this hour, the lake was pitch black. They quietly waited for fish to bite as they watched the sun come up. Patches of pink and orange clouds cast a fabric of magnificent reflections on the water. The sun created a golden hue through the trees. There was a slight haze on the water.

It was so quiet that a sense of calm came over them. Frank cherished moments like this, free from the stress of a grueling week at the police station. He savored chances to get away and concentrate on the serenity of the nature reserve. He also enjoyed being with his grandfather. He felt guilty for not spending enough time with him now, and made it up to him by taking him away for a few days.

Frank cast out his line and heard the gentle splash as it hit the water.

Gramps tossed his line out further and they were quiet. He looked back at Frank and asked, "How's Penny?"

"We broke up, Gramps."

"But you were nuts about each other."

"She couldn't deal with being with a cop. She didn't want to always worry if I'd get killed. I kept telling her that it's what I have to do."

"Maybe you should find a safer job."

"Gramps, you know I would never do that. Do you picture me sitting on my butt all day at some cushy job somewhere?"

"No, you wouldn't like that. You couldn't sit still long enough, I expect."

"You're right, I wouldn't last a week doing that kind of work."

"You can't work out a compromise?"

"It's over Gramps," he said flatly.

"You still love her don't you?"

"Yeah. She wants me to hang out with her boring coworkers. I was always telling her that she's not like that. She'd never listen."

"Why can't you hang out with those people?"

"They're snobs."

"She goes to police functions," Gramps pointed out.

"I didn't come here to talk about her." The line went taut and Frank reeled in a baby fish. He pried it off the hook and tossed it back in the water.

"I can't blame Penny for leaving you, Frank. You seem so preoccupied with work. You try to relax and not think about it, but I can tell you're worked up about something."

"How do you know?"

"I've got ESP. How's the Molloy case going?"

Frank guzzled coffee from the canteen and grunted, "It's keeping me busy, Gramps." He gave him an overview of what he discovered at the crime scene. "A neighbor saw this guy running away from the house. He had a gunshot wound in the shoulder."

Birds fluttered above and squawked across the lake. "It turns out that Molloy was married about twenty years ago. He got custody of his two kids. His ex-wife sneaked into his house one night and took them away. She was wanted for kidnapping."

There was a look of recognition in Gramps's eyes. "I remember the divorce case. It dragged on for months. The poor woman. She must've really been scared to have done such a thing."

"She was so scared, that they changed their names and lived on the run for years."

Gramps's eyes narrowed. "And he never found them?"

"Apparently not. It turns out the guy was a louse and the woman became an alcoholic in and out of hospitals. Her son, coincidentally, was seen outside his father's house the night he was hit on the head with the poker. He's the one who had the gunshot wound. It turns out that the 'burglar' is his long lost son."

His eyes widened. "Really? That's interesting."

Frank gazed across the glowing lake. A calm came over him that felt wonderful.

"The man's second wife has a business partner who lost heavily at the tracks and came to her husband, asking for a loan," Frank said after a long silence. "He refused to help him. But the dead guy had a life insurance policy that would have been enough for his wife's friend to repay his debts."

"Oh boy!"

"I thought it was sufficient motive for murder, but–" The line stiffened and he reeled in a Striped Bass. "Oh my God! It's a beauty!" He unhooked it and placed it in the bucket.

"We thought he did it, but he has an airtight alibi," he continued. "He was at a convenience store at the time the victim died. He was seen on the video surveillance camera at the time of Molloy's death. I spent days following the guy and it was all for nothing. Everybody seems to have an alibi."

"Maybe somebody's lying," Gramps suggested.

"I know somebody is lying, but I just can't figure out who it could be."

"It must be frustrating."

"It is, Gramps. Sometimes I get so close and then everything backfires."

"It'll come to you."

"Apparently the victim was a fisherman himself. He had all kinds of trophies around the room. And there were stuffed fish too. Apparently his son from his second marriage was jealous of his little brother. I can't blame him. The older son was away at school while the man took his youngest son on fishing trips. It's a classic case of sibling rivalry if I ever did see one."

"He does sound a bit jealous at that."

"You want to know what really frustrates me about the case?"

"What?"

"The guy got into a fight when his wife told him she wanted a divorce. She said he grabbed her arm and she ripped the sleeve of her dress when she pulled away. There's a scratch on his chest. All along, I thought she came back early from her business function, and got into another confrontation with him. I thought they must have struggled and that she scratched him real bad on the chest. A DNA test proved that she didn't do it."

Frank reeled in the line but there was nothing there, so he tossed it further out.

"I'm sorry I brought it up," Gramps said. "Just don't think about it for the rest of the day. It'll come to you."

Frank grinned and said, "Thanks, Gramps."

They changed the subject and concentrated on fishing. A few hours later, Frank pulled into the long driveway that led to the retirement community. Gramps got out and they slowly walked toward the entrance.

Frank hugged him and watched him walk around the bend, toward the lounge. On the way out, he smiled as wheelchair bound residents went by. The more fortunate residents pushed their walkers toward the dining room.

☆   ☆   ☆

CHAPTER 24

S pending the day fishing with his grandfather was all that Frank needed to get his energy flowing again. When he returned to work Monday morning, a lead came his way and he felt like he was on a roll. He was certain that he was close to solving the Molloy case after it went stagnant about a month ago.

Once again, he pored over the rather comprehensive list of telephone numbers that private detective, Luke Springer gave him. The calls were made from pay phones out of the area. Recent caller ID numbers from Molloy's home and office yielded no results, as well. He was on the verge of giving up, when one number caught his eye. He circled it and said, "Bingo."

He dialed the number and listened to a list of options for a medical office in West Chester.

He hung up and got online. He Googled the Marian R. Coleman Psychiatric Clinic and checked the address. The telephone number was a perfect match. He clicked on a staff member list, and smiled wryly. He found out all he needed to know.

*   *   *

When Thomas Smith's nurse quit, Yvonne took a few days off work to help her grandfather find another care giver. While she was in town, she ate dinner with Adam and Maggie. They kept her up to date about how his case was going. They all agreed that it was a major hassle. Donald Jenkins was right. It was circumstantial evidence.

A few days later, Adam went to check on his grandfather, while Yvonne went out to have coffee with Maggie. They had only been back at the apartment for a few minutes, when Detective Logan made a surprise visit.

He smiled and said, "I need to talk to you, Ms. Albright."

She let him in and closed the door. He sat on the sofa with the springs hanging out. She sat across from him.

"Have you found out anything?" she asked.

"I checked Seth Molloy's telephone records at his home and at the office and traced a number to an office outside of Philadelphia."

"That's nice, but what does it have to do with anything?"

"It has a lot to do with the case." He rattled off a telephone number and asked, "Does that number sound familiar?"

"No."

"I'll jog your memory then. I was able to get the street address for that number. It came from an extension at the same office where you work. This extension is from a private line there. Isn't it a coincidence that you just happen to work there?"

She pressed her fingers on the base of her nose and said, "Okay, I made the calls. But it doesn't prove anything."

"Threatening people is a serious offense, Ms. Albright. Especially if that person died under suspicious circumstances. Did Adam send you the notes? Did you work together on it? Start talking."

"Leave Adam out of it."

"Why should I? He confessed to sending them."

"Well, I helped him."

"You have an unusual hobby, Ms. Albright. Sending death threats."

"I told her to do it." Yvonne had been eavesdropping from the kitchen. She went into the living room and sat on a rickety straight back chair. "She didn't know what was inside the envelope. I just asked her to mail the letters as a favor."

"You don't have to cover up for me," Maggie told her.

Logan looked at her and asked, "Why did you do it?"

"We wanted to scare the old man," Yvonne answered for Maggie.

"Why?"

"Because of the horrible things he did to my mother," Yvonne said. "I swore I'd get him back."

"Does that include killing him?"

"That thought did cross my mind," Yvonne admitted. "We figured sending notes and making crank calls was punishment enough."

Logan looked from Yvonne to Maggie and said, "What did you hope to gain by resorting to scare tactics?"

"We wanted to scare him, that's all," Yvonne said.

"You scared him all right. He hired a private investigator to find out who was doing it. Sending threats of any kind is a felony."

Maggie's eyes widened in fear. "We—we—didn't think it would be so bad."

"It was just a stupid crank call," Yvonne said.

"You're both under arrest," Logan said gravely.

Maggie and Yvonne exchanged horrified looks.

Donald Jenkins spent an exhausting afternoon counseling both women separately. Maggie waited in her cell while Logan grilled Yvonne in the interrogation room, while the lawyer picked apart his case.

"You had no right arresting these poor women," Jenkins said. "So what if they made a few crank calls?"

"I had every right to arrest them, Mr. Jenkins. They deliberately reworded the phrases of a golden oldie to say *Today'll be the day that you die*. And then Seth Molloy was murdered. I've got a problem with that. And I'm sure a judge will too."

"They were shopping at the time Seth Molloy died. Witnesses can back them up. A judge will dismiss the case as the waste of time that it is."

Logan glared at the man. "I wouldn't count on it. A threat of any kind is a felony. When it's connected to an actual homicide, well–"

"The two cases have nothing to do with each other. These threats were just a coincidence."

"A coincidence huh? Well, Seth Molloy didn't take it just as a simple death threat or crank call. He hired a private detective to look into it."

"But this has nothing to do with the homicide investigation."

Logan leaned forward and said, "Well, we don't know that, do we? Maybe you were all in on it somehow."

Yvonne pursed her lips. "That is not true. We just did it to scare him. That's all."

"Well, we'll see what happens when it goes before a judge."

About fifteen minutes later, Jenkins escorted a visibly shaken Yvonne out of the room and took her back to her cell. It was now

Maggie's turn. She received a similar grilling from an extremely frustrated young detective who was tired of dealing with death threats and crank calls when he would rather be finding out the identity of the killer. Once again, Jenkins lectured Logan on what a sloppy job he was doing. The session ended about twenty minutes later. Logan went back to his desk and filled out paperwork to keep his mind off it.

He and Flosky had spent a long time checking the telephone list. What had started off as a great lead, wasn t so wonderful after all. Donald Jenkins would probably do some slick legal maneuvers and the women would get away with it.

About quarter to six, he called it quits for the day. He decided to work out at the gym for a little while to blow off steam. Then he'd grab something quick for dinner and unwind at his apartment. Anything to keep his mind off the case.

The next day, Frank got to the station early and pored over evidence from the Seth Molloy case once again. Then he comprised a time line and made some guesses about the time elements:

6 to 6:30 p.m.: Seth and Debbie's argument about divorce. He rips the sleeve on her dress. Picture frame gets broken in fight. Maybe she was angry that he had compromising photos of her with Raymond Sinclair.

7 to 7:45 p.m.: Seth Molloy takes shower and gets dressed.

7:45 to 8 p.m.: Seth hears a noise downstairs and goes to investigate, takes his gun with him. The burglar surprises him and knocks the weapon out of his hand. Seth gets hit on the head with a poker.

About 8 p.m.: Adam Jones (a.k.a. Robert Molloy) gets shot in the shoulder and a neighbor sees him fleeing Seth Molloy's house in a van. Before that, she heard a car backfiring, which must have been the sound of the gunshot. He sent the death threats. Maggie and Yvonne (a.k.a. Sarah Molloy) made crank phone calls.

Time of Death: Approximately 8 p.m.

Logan checked the time line for people with solid alibis.
6:15 p.m: Debbie takes Bonnie to art class early, goes to meet Raymond.
6:30 - 7:30 p.m.: Debbie and Raymond at Chamber of Commerce event at a restaurant with a lot of witnesses.

6 - 9 p.m.: Yvonne and Maggie went shopping at the King of Prussia Mall.

6:30 p.m.: Peter went to skateboard park near his school.

6:30 - 7 p.m.: Michael was the last person to see Seth alive and left approximately 7 p.m. to play video games with his friend down the street.

7 - 11 p.m.: Karl and Lynn Williams en route to their summer house at Rehoboth Beach, DE.

7:30 p.m.: Debbie went to her office. Alone for an hour. (Her house is 15 minutes away. She had plenty of time to go home, kill Seth, and get back in time to pick up Bonnie from her class on Main Street. There were no prints on the poker, so she still could have hit him on the head. I'm still not sure what to think about the scratch on his chest. Her DNA didn't match).

7:47 p.m.: Raymond was at a mini-mart about the time that Seth was murdered. He wouldn't have had time to go to the house and kill him.
8 - 10:15 p.m.: Peter came back from the park and was in his dorm studying with his roommate.

Logan looked at Joe Flosky and grimaced. "It's distressing, Joe. They've all got alibis. There's a piece missing. And I'll be damned if I know what that missing something is."

"We'll figure it out," Joe encouraged. "Maybe somebody's lying."
"People always lie for some reason or another."
"Maybe somebody's giving a fake alibi."
Logan tapped his pencil and reviewed his notes. "Yvonne and Maggie were seen on the video camera, right?"
"And so was Sinclair."
"Michael is the only one who was with his father before it happened. And he was close enough to walk to and from both houses."
"You aren't suggesting that he did it are you? He's just a kid."
"I'm just thinking of who had the easiest means of going back to the house, that's all. Debbie and Raymond were at least twenty minutes away."
"And they were with a lot of people," Joe reminded him. "And then she went to her office and was alone for a while."
"That's right, my friend. For once I would like to have a case that doesn't have anything to do with a dysfunctional family. What is the one common thread in this case?"
"Molloy had two wives."
"That's right. Does anything else stand out?"

"Molloy had a temper."

"He was also a wife beater."

"Do you think he was beating Debbie?" Joe wondered.

"I think so. Of course he was mistreating her. Does anything else stand out?"

"They're all secretive. Maybe there's something they aren't telling us. Or maybe there's something they're covering up."

"That's obvious, Joe. Somebody's lying and I'm going to find out who it is, if I have to pull teeth to make them talk."

❋   ❋   ❋

CHAPTER 25

Logan was shocked when the latest DNA test results came back. Michael was a match. Shortly after finding out the results, he met with Debbie and her son in an interrogation room.

Michael stared blankly at the test results, then back at Logan. "I don't know what you're talking about."

"The test proves that you scratched your father's chest," Logan said.

Debbie leaned forward and said, "You are antagonizing my son. This has nothing to do with my husband's murder. So what if he scratched Seth's chest?"

"When did it happen?"

"A few minutes before–before he died," Michael said.

"Why did you do it?"

Debbie clasped her hand to her mouth, pain deep in her eyes.

"Because," Michael fell silent.

There was a long, uncomfortable silence. Logan probed the boy's disturbed expression and repeated the question. "Why did you scratch him?"

"Because–because we–we got into a fight. He started yelling and–and it got out of hand."

"Did he hit you?"

Michael hung his head and said, "Yes."

"Why did he do it?"

"He was really upset about something that happened a few minutes earlier."

"What happened?" Logan persisted.

Michael looked at his mother and she said, "It's okay. You can tell him."

"My mom and dad just got into this really nasty argument before she left and he–and he was furious. I guess–I guess I just got in the way. After dinner, I went into his room to ask him if I could go over to Jeff's house. He took off his shirt to work out. I guess he was still upset about the fight and took it out on me. He started screaming and–and started pushing me around like a crazy person. I scratched his chest and got the hell out of there!"

Logan felt physically drained after taking Michael's statement. Debbie held her blubbering son in a tight embrace. He was trembling. They wept uncontrollably. She looked up at Logan and shot him an accusatory look.

He looked compassionately at her and said, "I'm so sorry, ma'am. I didn't mean for it to come to this. If there is anything I can do?"

"You have done quite enough," she said as she led the boy out of the interrogation room.

When he went back to his desk, Frank was visibly shaken. His face was ashen. Joe tapped his shoulder and said, "Is everything okay, pal?"

"What that kid went through is unspeakable. He's so brave." He handed Flosky the statement and Joe's eyes grew heavy as he read the grisly details of the physical and mental abuse that Seth unleashed on his boy.

Jeff was too busy playing his video game to give Logan much notice. He pressed on the joystick with all that it was worth and there was a loud bleeping noise as the head of a dragon blew off. When the game was over, he turned it off and looked up at the detective.

"What do you want?" he asked testily.

"I need to talk to you again about the night Mr. Molloy died," Logan said.

"What's there to know?"

"Michael said he was playing video games with you that night. Is there any time that you weren't around each other?"

"You're just trying to get him in trouble," Jeff said angrily.

"I'm just trying to get at the facts," Logan corrected. "Was there any point that night that you weren't together?"

Jeff shook his head. "Nah, we were at it all night, until his mom told us what happened."

"Think again. This is important."

"He was here. What can I say?"

Realizing that Jeff was a loyal friend and would cover for Michael, the weary detective decided to try a different tactic. "I checked telephone records. It looks like somebody was on the phone for a good twenty minutes that night."

"Really?"

"Weren't your parents out that night?"

"They had dinner with friends. What does that got to do with anything?"

"The phone was in use for twenty minutes." He read him the number and asked, "Does that number sound familiar?"

"It's a friend from school."

"So you admit talking to your friend?"

"Okay, so what does that prove?"

"Was Michael in the room with you?"

"No, I went in the other room to talk to him."

"So what you are basically saying is that you weren't together for a good twenty minutes, right?"

"Yeah, so what?"

"That gave Michael plenty of time to slip down the street and hit his father on the head and come back."

"If he had done that I would've heard the little man's voice go off when he opened the door. My folks have ADT."

"Maybe you didn't close the door all the way," Logan suggested.

Jeff shook his head and grunted. "We always keep it locked at all times."

"Well, maybe you forgot that night."

"It wouldn't have mattered anyway. I was sitting facing the hall. I would've seen him go out. You're just trying to get him in trouble because you don't know who else to blame. My folks read the papers and they talk about the case."

"Well, maybe the reporter doesn't get it right all of the time."

"You're just wasting your time. He couldn't have gone up the street and back in that amount of time."

"Maybe you should be a detective. From what you're saying, we obviously need all the help we can get."

"I don't like the idea of bothering poor saps that didn't do anything wrong," Jeff replied smartly.

"Then you wouldn't make a very good law enforcement officer. I think that he could have been in and out of here in that amount of time. You only live a few houses down."

"He was playing the game when I came back in the room."

Logan thanked him and was on his way out.

Logan checked room numbers and slipped in back of Cynthia Daley's ballet class. Parents were waiting to pick up their daughters. They smiled and engaged in small talk while they waited.

He quietly observed the young teacher. She had an overabundance of energy. Her eyes were powder blue and could easily light up a room. Her hair was blonde with braids down her back. Her cheeks were full and rosy.

When the class ended, the little girls squealed as they left the room. Cynthia went over to Logan and asked, "Can I help you?"

He smiled and showed her his badge. "Yes, you can. I'm here to ask about Bonnie Molloy."

She sighed and pursed her lips. "It's a shame about her father."

"The world isn't so nice sometimes," he sympathized. "That's kind of why I'm here, ma'am."

She looked at him wide-eyed and said, "You think I would know something?"

"Well, I actually thought you could clear something up for me. Bonnie told me she broke her leg in your ballet class a few weeks ago."

"Ballet injury?"

"Yes, the poor girl broke her leg while doing a routine in your class, didn't she?"

"I don't know what you're talking about! Bonnie didn't hurt herself in my class! You can ask my assistants. And you can ask parents who were here during the class! My children have never been hurt in my class!"

He opened his notepad and flipped back several pages. Then he reread his notes and waved his hand in the air.

"Oh my dear woman, I must have made a mistake! I must have assumed--it's another class all together! I'm sorry I upset you, Ms. Daley. Please accept my apologies."

"You can't just come in here and—"

Before she could finish speaking, he was out of there.

Logan hated to bother Raymond Sinclair again, but it had to be done.

"What do you want?" Sinclair moaned as he opened the door.

"There's something I overlooked. It was so obvious, I can't believe I missed it."

"What do you mean? You're talking in circles."

"I need to speak to Bonnie."

Debbie appeared at the top of the steps and said, "Leave her out of it. She's just a child."

"I only have a couple of questions. Then I'll be out of your hair."

"That's what you keep saying and you keep coming back like an annoying little bug," Raymond grumbled as they went upstairs.

"You've already put Bonnie through too much!" Debbie implored. "Is this necessary?"

"Seth was killed by a burglar," Raymond said.

Ignoring them, Logan made a beeline toward Bonnie's room. He went in and grinned widely. She was playing with a doll by the window and smiled when she saw him. Debbie stood quietly in the doorway.

"Hiah, Mr. Logan."

"Hi dear. I need to talk to you some more. Is that okay?"

"I guess so."

He knelt next to her and began with small talk. "Where's the cast?"

"They took it off a few days ago," she said.

"It must be nice to be able to walk right again."

"That's for sure. It kept itching and I couldn't scratch the itch."

"Oh, my." He looked at the shelf and complimented her on her toy collection.

Debbie came in and said, "I hoped you had gotten the information you needed, Detective Logan."

"You'll never know how many times detectives have to return to crime scenes Ms. Molloy. I'm sorry for the inconvenience."

"If you say or do anything to her, I'll talk to your superiors. Got that?"

"Go ahead."

Logan looked back at the girl and said, "Do you know what a fib is?"

"Yes."

"What does it mean?"

"It's when you don't tell the truth."

"That's right dear. Do you know what a half truth is?"

"It's when something isn't all the way true."

"Right," he said smoothly. "I have a little problem, dear. I found out some things that don't work together. You know like a puzzle. Things have to fit together like a puzzle. Do you understand?"

She looked up at him with her large blue eyes and said, "I think so."

"I talked to Mrs. Daley."

"She's really nice, isn't she?"

"Yeah, she's a nice lady," he agreed. "She told me you didn't break your leg in class. Would Mrs. Daley fib?"

"No."

"You didn't really break your leg in class, did you?"

She looked down and said, "No."

"How did you break your leg Bonnie?"

She rubbed the carpet and cradled her doll. "I fell down."

"How did you fall down?"

"Don't say another word, Bonnie!" her mother shouted.

"He's a nice man Mommy," she said.

He turned to face Debbie and said, "Mrs. Molloy, I talked to her ballet teacher. I know she didn't hurt her leg in class. Why don't you tell me how she broke it?"

Debbie's cheeks bloated and she cried, "That has nothing at all to do with this case! Why don't you try finding out who killed my husband, instead of--of harassing little girls!"

He looked back at Bonnie and said, "You know I'm your friend, don't you Bonnie?"

She nodded, still looking down.

"You can tell me. It's okay."

Tears streaked her face and he reached over to dry them.

"How did you hurt your leg Bonnie?"

She sniffed and said, "It was an accident--he didn't mean to--it--it just happened."

"What do you mean Bonnie?" he asked gently. "Did someone push you? Who hurt your leg?"

She turned around and played with her dolls.

"Who hurt you Bonnie? You can tell me, I'm your friend."

"You're upsetting her Detective Logan!" Debbie screamed. "Get out of here!"

He knelt down beside the child and repeated, "Who hurt your leg?"

"Daddy!" she wailed.

"What did he do?"

She raced out of the room shouting, "He pushed me down the steps!"

* * *

CHAPTER 26

Debbie was seething with anger. She wrapped her arms around Bonnie and dried her tears.

"Now see what you've done?" Debbie wailed. "I want you out of here right now!"

"I'm sorry, ma'am. I know you're upset."

She gritted her teeth and said, "Upset doesn't quite cover it. You have no right coming in here and upsetting my little girl like that."

"I'll go, but I need to talk to you later. So long."

Raymond followed him out the door and had it out with him. Debbie watched Logan pull onto the street and disappear from view around the bend. When Raymond came back in, his face was beet red.

"The nerve of that man!" He went over to Bonnie and ran his hand through her hair. "Are you all right, pumpkin?"

She sniffled and said, "Mommy promised to get us ice cream."

Raymond smiled. "Ice cream always makes people feel better."

Debbie shook her head at him. "I can't believe what that man is capable of."

"He should know better than harassing little girls," Raymond said. "I'll go over his head and issue a complaint."

"Come on, who wants to go for ice cream?"

"Let's go!" Bonnie squealed.

A back log of tests from other cases delayed the results of other evidence gathered at the Seth Molloy crime scene. When a purple stain found on Seth's robe was examined, Logan started putting the puzzle pieces together. A week later, he went back to the Molloy home when he had had time to gather all the evidence together. He rang the doorbell but there was no answer. He went to the back of the house and saw Debbie and Raymond sitting at a table under the shade of an umbrella. They were drinking tea and reading the newspaper. The kids were horsing around in the swimming pool. He opened the gate and walked onto the deck. It looked like they were getting ready for the fourth of July. Decorations were hanging up. An American flag hung on a post.

"Good afternoon, Mrs. Molloy," he said.

She looked up at him and scowled. "What do you want?"

"I'm sorry to bother you again, but I've got some things to discuss with all of you."

"You've already caused enough trouble," Raymond said. "Leave us alone."

"I can't do that. I need to talk to the boys. It's urgent."

He walked over to the deep end and waved at Peter and Michael. They climbed the ladder and went over to deck chairs with their towels draped on them. They wrapped them around their waists and sat down next to the adults. Logan pulled up a chair facing them. They watched Bonnie splashing her hands in the water. She squealed with joy.

"Are you coming in, Mommy?"

Debbie smiled and said, "In a little bit, honey. Just stay in the shallow end, okay?"

"Okay, Mommy."

Debbie looked back at Logan and asked, "Did you find out who killed my husband?"

"It looks that way, ma'am." He looked from Debbie to Raymond to the boys. "I've read and reread my notes and one thing sticks out. A neighbor heard a car backfiring about eight o'clock. Tests indicated that your husband died about that time. What she thought was a car backfiring, was really a gunshot in your back window."

"That's when Seth shot at the burglar," Raymond said.

"That's what the killer wanted us to think. But we all know it wasn't a botched burglary attempt, and I'll tell you why. His fingerprints were on the gun, but tests proved that he didn't fire the weapon. There were no gun powder burns on his hand. At first, I thought there was a struggle, and the gun slipped out of his hand. But that isn't true. I think he was so paranoid that somebody was out to get him that he carried his weapon with him everywhere he went."

They all nodded their heads in agreement.

"The killer hit him with the poker and he fell and hit his head. The killer placed the gun on the floor, a few feet from his body and made it look like Seth caught him in the middle of committing the robbery. He knocked over chairs and shelves to make it look like a struggle. Then he put a TV and some other things on the kitchen floor. He broke the window with a baseball bat that we found lying on the ground out back. And then he fired a couple of shots at the kitchen door, not realizing that he shot a man who happened to be at the wrong place at the wrong time.

"There was a scratch on his chest. All along, I thought that you scratched him that night, Mrs. Molloy, but I was wrong." He looked at Michael and said, "The DNA test proved that Michael did it."

Michael hung his head in shame.

"You were all covering up a dirty little family secret. Physical and mental abuse. When I first saw Bonnie's cast, I didn't think anything about it. But there was more to it, wasn't there? Michael, you neglected to tell me what your father did to her."

"I couldn't talk about it."

"What happened?" Logan asked calmly.

Michael closed his eyes and rocked his body to-and-fro as he relayed the horrible events that occurred a few days before his father's death. Seth was so drunk that he started beating on Debbie. Bonnie ran out of the room in tears. Michael pushed him out of the way to protect his mother. Seth beat him repeatedly until there was blood all over the place.

"My mom was just standing there screaming. It got really crazy, like something out of a nightmare. And then he ran out of the room. And then–and then we heard a loud noise. Bonnie was shouting and crying. We went into the hall and saw her lying on the hall floor."

"What happened?"

"Seth pushed her down the steps," Debbie answered for him. "I took them to the ER–and the doctor knew. He encouraged me to contact the police and file an abuse report. That's when I made up my mind. I decided to divorce him."

"The bastard!" Raymond exclaimed. "If I'd have been there, I would have killed him on the spot!"

"Me too," agreed Peter.

"Which leads me to you, Peter," Logan said facing him. "Did he do it to you?"

He looked down and mumbled, "Yes."

"Don't feel ashamed. You aren't the only one's he did this to. Your father did this to your half-brother, Rob and your half-sister, Sarah. His ex-wife took off with them. It took some time to track them down, because their mother changed their names. They lived on the run for twenty years. When I found them, Rob admitted that his father, the one and only Seth Molloy had beaten him when he was a child. It would have continued if his mother hadn't gotten them out of the house."

Peter groaned and buried his face in his hands. "No!"

"How long had he been beating you?"

"Since I was a little kid," Peter admitted.

"You were right, Peter. Your father wanted you out of the way. You were too big and could defend yourself. With you out of the way, you couldn't stop him from hurting the rest of your family, right?"

Peter nodded and said, "That's why I was so upset the day I talked to my mom on the phone. Michael texted me right after they got back from the ER the night before. I was upset that I wasn't there to protect them from him."

"You felt guilty," Logan said. "It's perfectly understandable."

"I kept insisting on transferring to Townsend High, but he refused."

"He would never listen to anything I said either," Debbie added.

Logan looked from Debbie to Raymond and then to the boys and said, "I'll tell you what happened next. You were so upset,

Peter, that you decided to confront him. Isn't that true? You went to the skateboard park to give yourself an alibi. I asked some kids there that know you. Instead of going back to the campus, you rode home. Somehow you knew that he was the only one in the house that night. I'm sure neighbors would have said something if they saw you coming or going. They were probably so busy with their own lives that they didn't pay attention to what was going on outside their homes."

Anger flashed in Peter's eyes. "That's impossible! I was studying in my dorm a half an hour away. Todd and I were studying together."

"It's true. You were in your dorm—about an hour later. But you had been at home before that, waiting for Seth to come downstairs."

"You don't have any proof."

"That's where you're wrong, Peter. Forensics is a fascinating science. Lab technicians discovered a purplish stain on your father's robe."

"What does that prove? He probably spilled something on it."

"It didn't come from anything he ate or drank. It was a saliva stain. Your DNA swab was a perfect match. It places you at the scene of the crime."

"That doesn't prove anything," Raymond was quick to point out. "It could have been an old stain."

"Lab technicians figured out that it was a fresh stain. It came from grape chewing gum. Here's what I think happened. You came to talk to him alone. You got into a fight and spit on him. And then you hit him on the head with the poker and made it look like he stopped a burglar in progress. It wasn't a car backfiring that the neighbor heard. It was actually the gunshot through the kitchen window. Your half-brother, Rob, really was at the wrong place at

the wrong time. He got a bullet in the shoulder and was seen fleeing from the house in his van."

There was a long, uneasy silence.

"No one wanted the dreadful secret to come out," Logan continued. "And you would all stick up for each other. Peter, the DNA
evidence links you to the crime."

"Okay, I did it!" Peter admitted.

"Peter, no!" Debbie screamed. "I did it! He was a bastard! Do
you know what it was like living with him?"

"Why don't you tell me?" Logan said.

"He was domineering. I could never please him. We had to walk
on eggshells around him. He–he was unpredictable. We never knew
what would set him off. When he got drunk, he took out his anger
on us. I had to make him pay for all the pain that he caused. I
scratched Seth during our argument. You even commented on my
ripped blouse. Remember, Detective Logan? He wouldn't let go,
so I scratched his chest. I thought he was going to force himself on
me. I had to do something. I knew what he was doing, and I had to
stop it once and for all. That's why I left the restaurant early. I took a
shortcut to the house. He was downstairs reading when I got home.
We had another argument about the divorce. He forced himself on
me. I tried to push him off, but he wouldn't let up. So I--I hit him
on the head with the poker. I was so upset, I went up to his room
and got his gun and shot at the back window and--and made it look
like he walked in on a burglar. Then I went to pick up Bonnie."

"Nice try, ma'am," Logan said. "The purple stain on Seth's robe
matches Peter's DNA sample."

"Oh Peter," she wailed.

"Mom, you can't lie to protect me. I won't let you take the
blame. There's no way of getting away from it now. He's got me

where he wants me." He looked back at Logan and said, "I had to do it. I was afraid he'd kill them."

"But I did do it!" she insisted.

Raymond rubbed her shoulders and looked sadly at Peter.

"You're covering up for him," Logan said. "It's no use. The truth has come out. Don't cover up for a crime you didn't commit. You lied to protect Michael when I told you that Seth's chest had been scratched. It is true that your dress sleeve ripped during your fight with Seth. You figured you could get away with telling me you scratched him. You'd even lie and say you killed him. You don't want Peter to go to prison. I really do believe you would do anything for your children, including covering up this dirty little secret. You would have probably liked to have taken it to your grave. But there is no way to get around it."

She burst into tears, realizing, to her horror that there was no way she could protect her child. Although she knew the horrible things Seth had done, she couldn't stop it. Lying to Detective Logan was her only way of helping him.

"No, no, no," she whimpered.

Logan stared Peter down and said, "You had motive. And you had the perfect opportunity to do it. And we've got the scientific evidence to back it up. Start talking."

"All right, I guess I don't have a choice," Peter said flatly. He went on to describe the awful chain of events that transpired that night, while his mother blubbered in the background...

When Seth came downstairs, he was surprised to see Peter sitting on the reclining chair in the family room with his gloves on.

"'What are you doing here?'" he asked in alarm.

"I want to talk to you about what you did to Bonnie."

"You should be at school." He put the wine glass on the end table next to the sofa, and laid the gun next to it.

"I should be at school so you can beat the hell out of everybody! You can do anything you want to them as long as I'm out of the picture. Isn't that right? I'm stuck there so I can't protect them. That's what you wanted. That's why you sent me there." He got to his feet and stood practically nose to nose with his father. "With me stuck at school, nobody's here to stop you from beating the shit outta everybody!"

"Go back to your dorm and shut up about it!"

"No, I won't keep quiet! Not this time! You could've killed Bonnie! What's wrong with you? You're a sick bastard!"

Seth hit Peter so hard that he fell on the floor. He put his right foot on his son's chest and hovered over him. Peter spit on him. Purple saliva from his chewing gum spewed onto his father's robe.

"I'll talk to the police," Peter said out of breath.

"Nobody'll believe you. Everybody likes me. They'll think you're a lying punk. You're a punk!"

Peter rolled over and managed to knock him off balance. He scrambled to his feet and got in his face.

"If you hurt Bonnie again, I'll kill you!"

"You're too much of a puss to do it."

Peter spit on him again and shouted, "I'll see to it that you never hurt anybody again!"

Seth backed his way toward the fire place and leaned down to pick up a poker. He swung it at him and Peter dodged out of the way.

"You're a sick bastard!" Peter shouted through tears. "What's wrong with you?"

Seth swung at Peter's chest. He hit him repeatedly until Peter dropped to his knees. He reached for the other poker and waited...

Seth towered over him, taunting him.

"You're a worthless piece of garbage!" Seth hollered. "I should've gotten you out of here years ago! Always complaining! Always angry! Well, buddy boy, life's crappy! Get in the real world you spoiled son of a bitch!" He swung inches away from Peter's head but missed. Peter rolled out of the way and sprang to his feet.

"Get the fuck away from me!" Peter screeched. "You won't hurt them again! I won't let you!" With a fit of rage, he hit Seth on the head.

Blood spurted from Seth's head. The poker slipped out of his hand and he teetered toward Peter a moment before falling on his back. There was a loud crunching sound as his skull made contact with the brick fire place floor.

Peter watched the events unfold with wild-eyed horror. It was over in a flash. He didn't take time to see if he was dead or alive. He knew he had to get out of there.

His heart was racing. Perspiration soaked his shirt. His face was hot and moist.

"Oh my God!" he shouted repeatedly. "What've I done? I've gotta think!"

He ran his fingers through his tussled blond hair and looked around the room. He took several deep breaths and tried to remain calm. He rambled incoherently.

"He was here by himself...his gun...it was just a thief..."

He picked up the gun next to the sofa and stood in the entry-way leading to the kitchen. He aimed it at the window and fired a couple of shots. He was so preoccupied with the gravity of the situation that he didn't see the man standing outside the door.

He hurried into the family room and laid the weapon on the floor, a few feet from his father's body. He turned chairs on their sides. He knocked over a knickknack shelf and glass bric-a-bracs shattered on the floor. He moved across the room with lightening speed and hauled the TV into the kitchen. He put it on the floor and hurried back into the den to get the laptop.

He looked around the room to see if there was anything he forgot. The wall clock read 8:17 p.m. He ran out the back door, grabbed the baseball bat, and hit the window. He tossed it on the patio and darted toward his Harley. He pushed it toward the front of the house, and looked up and down the street to make sure no one would see him. No one was there. Street lights were on. Lights were on in people's houses. He pushed it a half a block and hopped on. He revved the engine and sped around the bend...

Everyone sat in stunned silence when Peter finished telling about what happened. The only noise was that of Bonnie splashing around in the swimming pool.

Peter was so emotionally distraught, that his body was shaking. Tears streaked his cheeks and he wept uncontrollably. Debbie went over and put her arms around him. "Oh, Peter, I'm so sorry," she said through tears. "We'll get through this somehow."

"The hell you had to go through," Logan said softly. "It's so sad that it had to come to this."

"I did everything for you all," Peter said. "I only wish I had done something sooner."

Michael sniffled and said, "What else could you have done?"

"I could've called the cops."

"Nobody would've believed you," Michael said.

Logan nodded his agreement. "Your father was such a good actor, I don't think anybody would've believed you, either." He looked back at Peter and said, "How long did it take from the time you fired the shots to the time you left?"

"About fifteen minutes," Peter replied hoarsely.

"Mrs. van Horn could have easily mistaken the gunshots for a car backfiring." He reached for his handcuffs and said, "I'm sorry Peter, but you're under arrest for the murder of your father, Seth Molloy." He cuffed him and read him his rights.

"I didn't mean to do it," he said as they walked away.

"I did it!" Debbie shouted repeatedly.

"This is an outrage!" Raymond cried. "I'll get you the best lawyer money can buy."

They raced to the front yard and Raymond wrapped his arms around her as they watched Logan put Peter in the car and drive down the street. Michael stood with his hands straight to his side, too stunned for words.

"Raymond! Raymond! He's just arrested my boy!"

✧   ✧   ✧

CHAPTER 27

Defense Attorney Tim Boyer adjusted his wire-rimmed glasses as he pored over the evidence in the Seth Molloy case. In his late forties, he was a formidable figure with broad shoulders and an iron-muscled physique. He had a square jaw and large blue eyes hidden behind the glasses. He had feathered brown hair, with graying temples that offered the only clue to his age. He played football at Penn State in his glory days. He could still play the game with college kids half his age without having to take a rest break like a lot of his former teammates.

Boyer worked with Seth about fifteen years earlier. Debbie only knew him from occasional office parties, but she knew he was a good lawyer. He had a reputation for fairness, but he could also be tough. Right now, that was what Peter needed. Peter and Debbie quietly listened to Boyer and Detective Logan go over the evidence. When Logan left, Boyer spent two hours developing a strategy.

"What are my chances?" asked Peter.

"I will argue that you acted in self defense," Boyer said. "After years of abuse, I can make the jurors feel sympathy for you."

"It shouldn't have had to come to this," Debbie muttered. "I should've packed up and moved the kids out a long time ago."

"Sometimes that's easier said than done, Debbie," Boyer said. He looked back at his notes and said, "We'll need Michael to testify. Is he up to it?"

She shuttered and said, "I guess."

"Well, maybe we can get Seth's ex-wife and children from his previous marriage to testify."

She shook her head and said, "I can't believe he did this to another family too."

"He left a trail of broken lives," Boyer said. "He fooled a lot of people, including me. But he won't hurt anybody else. You've got to remember that."

They continued working on strategies until about four o'clock. A guard appeared at the door and told them it was time to take Peter back to his cell. Debbie wrapped her arms around her son and kissed his forehead.

He squeezed her hands and said, "We'll get through this."

"I love you," she said choking on her tears.

When they were gone, Boyer escorted her out. They went to a lounge where Michael and Raymond were waiting. Michael looked at her bloodshot eyes and knew that she had been crying. Her expression was blank. He hugged her.

"It'll be all right," the boy assured her.

Raymond put his arm around her waist and escorted her out of the police station. "Come on, let's go home and order pizzas or something."

Michael trailed behind them.

Peter appeared at a preliminary hearing the next morning. Raymond Sinclair watched with intense concentration, as Peter conferred with Tim Boyer. It was so hot in the courtroom, Raymond's shirt felt moist. Michael rubbed his mother's arm to help calm her down. The judge listened carefully as prosecutor Edward Welsh reviewed the evidence of the homicide investigation. Welsh was tall and thin with a lantern jaw. His face was pale with short gray hair.

Logan agreed to speak on Peter's behalf. "Your Honor, due to the tragic circumstances involving this case, I beg you to grant leniency. His father had been physically abusing him for years, and there is sufficient evidence that he acted in self defense. Years of psychological and physical abuse took their toll on the young man."

"I'm sure that everyone involved will take that into consideration, Detective Logan," the judge said.

When Adam and Yvonne spoke, they were both in agreement. Seth had beaten them up when they were children. Lynn provided the necessary photographs to collaborate their stories. Welsh played a tape recording that Peter secretly recorded of one of his father's rants. Everyone could hear Seth screaming and breaking things. They could hear how violent he was.

Raymond had heard Debbie's horror stories, but was now witnessing them first hand. He leaned toward her and whispered, "Are you sure you can sit through this?"

She choked back tears and said, "I have to do this for Peter. It'll be okay."

"You're so brave."

Lynn was experiencing the same feelings of fear and anguish from three rows back. Karl held her hand and spoke calmly. "I'm so sorry you have to go through this all over again."

She sniffled and said, "It has to be done. The things that poor boy had to go through."

"It really isn't fair," whispered Karl.

Welsh produced self portraits that Peter photographed and hid in a shoe box in his closet. There were close up images of his chest and torso after Seth beat him. Another one showed a close up shot of his face. He had a black eye and bruised lips.

"At the time, I told people that I was jogging in the woods and slipped on ice," Peter admitted. "Sometimes I said I got hurt playing sports."

He paused to wipe tears from his eyes. "I had to wear hoodies to hide the bruises on my face and neck. And I–and I always took my showers and got dressed last. I didn't want my teammates to see the marks on my body."

A few minutes later, a psychiatrist suggested that kind of behavior was exhibited by a boy or girl who was a victim of physical abuse. They were still going over evidence, when Logan had to leave. He went up to Debbie and whispered, "If there's anything I can do, let me know."

She sniffled and said, "Thank you."

He left the courtroom feeling physically drained.

Peter was charged with voluntary manslaughter, and would be tried as an adult. The judge set the trial date for October.

The next day, Peter's high school portrait was on the front page of Townsend's weekly newspaper, the *Times-Sentinel*. The headline read: "TEEN ARRESTED FOR MURDERING FATHER."

By Kim Weston

TOWNSEND–A local teen was arrested Tuesday afternoon for the murder of his father three months ago. Peter

Molloy, 16, of Townsend, has been accused of allegedly bludgeoning his father, Seth, to death on April 21ˢᵗ.

Seth Molloy was a prosecutor in Townsend, and a pillar of the community. His wife Debbie came back from picking up their daughter from a class on Main Street, and discovered his body in the family room later that night. According to the police, Molloy died from being hit on the head with a poker. His gun was found a few feet from his body. Peter allegedly fired the weapon to make it look like a failed burglary attempt. Household items were on the kitchen floor. A bullet hole was in the kitchen door.

Seth's son from a previous marriage, Robert, 27, was shot in the shoulder as he was spotted fleeing the premises. Authorities believed he was Peter's accomplice.

"DNA evidence proved that he never stepped foot in the house," said Defense Attorney Donald T. Jenkins. "He was just in the wrong place at the wrong time."

Robert Molloy faces terroristic threat charges. Prior to Seth's murder, he had been receiving death threats. In May, the police searched Robert's apartment and found cut up magazines that were apparently used for the death threats. Detective Frank Logan of the Townsend Police Department declined to comment on the matter at this time.

Peter Molloy pleaded not guilty to voluntary manslaughter. He will be tried as an adult. The trial is set for October.

Lynn Williams had to deal with her own legal demons. She always knew that someday she would have to face up to her kidnapping charges. Her trial date was scheduled for the first week of August. When the truth came out about their true identities, she spent many long hours discussing the case with Donald Jenkins. Adam and Yvonne lent their moral support. Karl and Maggie listened quietly and offered helpful suggestions.

While Jenkins reviewed files, Lynn read the newspaper article about Peter Molloy's case. Tears rolled down her cheeks when she saw the part about Adam's arrest. When she finished reading it, she grimaced and laid it on Donald's conference room table.

"It's such a shame that he ruined the lives of another family," she said.

"It's a tragedy," agreed Jenkins. "I can't believe he got away with abusing his second wife's kids too."

Lynn wiped her tears and said, "He caused so much pain and suffering." Then she relayed the whole ugly story of the horrible things Seth did to her during the custody hearings.

"Did he hurt you too, Yvonne?"

"Yes!" she cried. "But Adam got the brunt of it."

"The damage was already done when I got them out," Lynn said. "I was too late and I've always blamed myself for it. Drinking helped ease the guilt. Living on the run, always scared to look over your shoulder does something to a person. I lived every day in constant fear that he'd find us and put me in prison where I couldn't protect the kids. I think I would have died if that had happened. I would've killed him before he got a chance to hurt them again! If I wound up in prison, my father would have taken care of the children."

She reached for Karl's hand and said, "I put you through hell for years, Karl. But you've been patient and stuck by me. You didn't deserve to be treated the way I treated you." She looked back at Jenkins and said, "Every time I was hospitalized, I planned how I'd kill Seth if I saw him again. I had sufficient motive for all the pain he caused the children and me. So I asked Adam to do me a favor. I wanted him to scare Seth. And for the record, I want to let it be known, that I told them to send the threatening notes and make the crank calls."

"You don't have to do it, Ma," Adam said. "I made the calls and I'll face up to the charges." He looked at Jenkins and said, "How serious is it?"

"A felony is a serious charge," Jenkins said. "But let's concentrate on your mother's case first, shall we?"

"Now that everybody knows our true identities, will I go to jail for kidnapping my kids?" Lynn asked.

"It's up to jurors, Mrs. Williams," Jenkins said. "They'll have to look at the circumstances leading up to your taking them, and look at your mind set."

"I was frightened out of my skull!" Lynn exclaimed.

"I bet you were," agreed Jenkins.

"You live your life so secretively for so long that your fake name becomes your personality," Yvonne said. "I often wondered if I did something to deserve it. I looked for a reason to justify it but I never could."

"It's never the fault of the victim," Jenkins said. "He was a sick man. If he had sought treatment, he might have gotten himself straightened out."

Yvonne burst into tears and hurried out of the room.

"Will she be okay?" Jenkins asked.

"She gets that way sometimes," Adam said. "She thinks she is actually Yvonne." He went out to see if she was all right. Maggie went with him.

"All these secrets that have been buried for years," Lynn said. "Secrets that are better left alone. Too many lives have been ruined because of that monster. Peter did the world a favor by doing him in. I only wish I did it."

Adam, Yvonne, and Maggie came back ten minutes later. Focus shifted on their terroristic threat charges. About six o'clock Jenkins drew the session to a close. Lynn reached for Karl's hand and they followed everyone else out the door.

They picked up where they left off bright and early the next morning. This time, Tim Boyer joined the talk with the Molloys and Raymond Sinclair. Logan went over the evidence with them. They gathered in a conference room in Donald Jenkins's office. Peter got off on bail and wore an ankle bracelet monitor. When he entered the room, Peter's eyes automatically were drawn to Adam.

"Adam, meet your half-brother, Peter Molloy," Jenkins said. "He's the one that shot you in the shoulder the night your father was killed."

Adam and Peter exchanged knowing glances. For years, Adam had thought about killing Seth Molloy for all the pain and suffering he caused his family, but Peter did it. He felt sorry for him.

Everybody introduced themselves and made small talk.

"Did he beat you too?" Peter asked Adam.

"Yeah," he said. "It took guts to do what you did. You'll be okay. I'm sure they'll say you acted in self defense."

It wasn't long before they swapped horror stories.

"I can't believe that any human being could do such a thing," Maggie said. "He got what he deserved."

"I only wish I had thought of it about twenty years ago," Lynn said.

"What will happen to Peter?" Michael asked. "Will he have to go to prison?"

"It will be up to the jurors," Boyer said.

"It isn't fair!" Michael protested. "He was just trying to protect us from our dad!"

"The no good scum!" Adam cried. "I wish I had hit him!"

"Did you see Peter that night Adam?" asked Logan.

"Yes," he admitted.

"So you risked going to jail to protect somebody you didn't know?"

"He did me a favor. It's something I wanted to do for a long time. I didn't know him, but I knew what he was going through."

"What will happen to him?" Yvonne wondered.

"I'm sure Tim could prove that he was suffering from years of psychological torment," Logan said. "You can all attest to that. I say it was a clear act of self defense."

"Will he have to go to jail?" Lynn asked.

"I hope not."

"But he's so young," Maggie said. "Life's pretty crappy sometimes. He never had a chance. His father was abusing him."

"That's the key to the case," Boyer pointed out.

Debbie hung her head and looked like she was about to cave in or start sobbing. Michael patted her shoulder to comfort her. "It shouldn't have come to this," she said. "I think we'll all be in need of counseling."

"I can recommend some counselor's," Logan said. "There are police psychiatrists and referrals."

"You've done quite enough," Debbie said with a definite bite to her tone.

"Maybe it will help to open up about it," Logan suggested. "I know of some good support groups."

Debbie nodded in agreement. "Maybe we should try them. We'll need something to get our lives back on the right track."

Michael patted his mother's arm and said, "It'll be okay. We'll get through this."

It was at that moment that Debbie realized how grown up her younger son was.

Logan left them to continue working on a strategy.

Thomas Smith leaned on his walker and took slow, calculating steps into the courtroom. He edged toward the closest seat and sat down with effort. Lynn was up front, conferring with Jenkins. He glanced at the prosecution table. Prosecutor Jared Meyers hovered over a pile of paperwork and consulted with his colleagues. Both men were middle-aged and wore dark suits. Meyers hair was dyed jet black. Large wire-rimmed glasses hung over a small nose. There was a serious expression on his face. It looked like he never had any fun. A red-headed woman in her mid-thirties worked feverishly alongside them. She had on a beige pants suit. She wore horn rimmed glasses and wore very little makeup. Her hair was in a bun, and she looked as severe as her coworkers. The judge was an African American woman about forty-five. She was probably a mother. Maybe she would be more sympathetic.

Thomas studied the expressions on the jurors faces, hoping they would identify with the plight his daughter had to go through for so many years. The fear and anxiety of the custody hearing came flooding back to Thomas, when Jared Meyers rose to make his opening statement. This time, however, she did not look like a fragile wreck. Life on the run had hardened her. She was worldly-wise now. She knew what had to be done.

Meyers painted her as an evil woman who snatched her small children from the safety of their home, and took off to parts unknown. Her reckless disregard of her children's safety was inexcusable. The children were left with psychological scars that never healed. She broke the law and should be punished to every extent of the law.

Donald Jenkins depicted a frightened young woman who did whatever she had to do to provide for the safety of her children. Seth Molloy was a monster, and she was fearful of what he might do to them if he gained custody.

Thomas's eyes welled with tears as he was forced to relive the painful memories. Watching his daughter's melt down after the judge awarded custody to Seth was a horrible experience. This time it was different. He remained hopeful.

When it was her turn to testify, she took her seat and used her real name when she was sworn in. She felt an unbelievable sense of comfort to see her father in the gallery. His look of encouragement gave her the strength to proceed.

"For the record, you used the name Amelia when you were sworn in," Meyers began. "But that is not the name you go by, correct?"

"That's right."

"For about twenty years, you have gone by another name, isn't that right?"

"Yes."

"What name do you go by?"

"Lynn Jones-Williams. Five years ago, I married Dr. Karl Williams."

"Did you legally change your name?"

"I took my husband's last name when we got married. But I still go by Lynn."

"Why did you change your name to Lynn?"

"So my ex-husband couldn't find me."

Meyers turned to face the jurors and reminded them of her kidnapping charge. That date twenty years ago was stamped in her memory forever. Of course she remembered where she was that night, and why she was there. She had to get the children away from Seth!

"Where did you go?" Meyers asked.

"Out west. We lived in Phoenix for a while. Then we moved to Santa Fe. And then on to Nashville for a few months."

"The whole while you were gone, did you have any care in the world what your ex-husband was going through?"

"No, I did not."

"You put your children in danger, living on the run. Deplorable conditions. On the run from the police. You changed your name and their names. Didn't you fear for their welfare?"

"It's haunted me for years," she admitted.

"Did you let them play or have friends?"

She swallowed hard and wiped her tears. "That is something that I'll regret for the rest of my life. But—but I couldn't let them hang out with friends that often...I was so scared that a cop would recognize them."

"Did you keep them in the house when they weren't in school?"

"Most of the time. But we did take walks in the park. Sometimes they went riding on their bikes. But it was always near the trailer. I always had to be with them when we went out."

Meyers addressed the jurors. "Can you tell me what kind of life that is to treat your own children like prisoners? Some people would say that you were a heartless mother."

"I did what I had to do!" she insisted.

"Did you ever try to contact Seth Molloy and let him know that his children were okay?"

"No."

"They were his children too. And you ripped them away from him. Isn't that true?"

"I had to do it or he'd–he'd get them!"

"During the testimony, it came out that you had a bit of a drinking problem." He read a transcript from the custody hearing from twenty years ago. "Isn't it true that you told a friend that you had a little too much to drink at a party?"

"Yes."

"Did you go to the emergency room?"

"Yes."

"Why did you go there?"

"I had a broken collar bone."

"Didn't you tell a nurse that you tripped and fell down?"

"Yes."

"Did they mention abuse?"

"Yes."

"What did you tell them?"

"I denied it," she admitted. "I said I tripped and fell down the steps."

"And they believed you?"

"I don't think so."

"So, you admitted under oath that you got hurt due to your own carelessness?"

"Yes."

"Are you telling us now, after all these years, that you were lying under oath?"

"Yes."

"Why should we believe anything you have to say?"

She admitted that she was terrified about what Seth would do to her. He had convinced her that no one would believe her.

"Nothing further."

Donald Jenkins went up to her and said, "Do you love your children, Mrs. Williams?"

"Yes, of course I do."

"You would do just about anything for them, correct?"

"Yes."

He looked at the jurors, then turned his attention back on her. "Parents have gut instincts to protect their children. You testified that you did it to protect them. The situation must have been really bad for you to kidnap your own children."

She said she was so frightened of Seth, that she feared for her life and the lives of her children.

Then she relayed the whole, ugly story of the horrible physical abuse inflicted on poor little Robby, when Seth was drunk and angry.

"Did you take care of Robby's injuries on your own?" asked Jenkins.

"I tried to fix him up the best I could."

"What were the extent of the injuries?"

"Robby had cuts on his chest and torso. His lips were swollen. He had a black eye."

"Did you report the injuries to the police?"

"No."

"Why not? Those injuries were obviously the result of physical abuse. How could you fool people so well?"

"I dressed him in long sleeve shirts and pants. Turtlenecks and sweaters. I learned how to hide it."

"Why didn't you call the police?"

"Because Seth told me that nobody would believe that he did it."

"Was this brought up at the divorce proceedings?"

"No."

"If it had been, I'm sure that you would have gained custody of the children."

Jared Meyers rose and said, "Objection. Speculation."

The judge ruled in favor of the prosecutor and ordered Jenkins's last statement be stricken.

"Was Seth a good father?"asked Jenkins.

"He was a strict disciplinarian," she answered sharply.

"Would he have been the better care provider?"

She shook her head. "It would have been a shame if they had been raised by him."

"Did you fear for their safety?"

"All the time. I feared for their lives."

"Nothing further."

When the prosecution and defense rested their cases, jurors listened intently to their closing statements. After reviewing the testimonies of Amelia and her children, they went on to discuss evidence from Debbie and her kids. They looked at photographs of Peter's injuries, and listened to the secret tapes of Seth Molloy's rants. They were all in agreement. Amelia Molloy-Williams acted in the best interest of her children. Twenty years living on the run, under the assumed name of Lynn Jones was suffering enough. She was found not guilty and her charges were dropped.

The next day, there was a photo of Amelia Molloy-Williams exiting the courthouse with Donald Jenkins next to her. The headline read: "ON THE LAM MOTHER FOUND NOT GUILTY OF KIDNAPPING HER KIDS"

By Kim Weston

TOWNSEND–On Tuesday afternoon, Amelia Molloy-Williams was found not-guilty of kidnapping her children 20 years ago, after a heated custody proceeding. Her then husband Seth was awarded custody of their seven-year-old son, Robert, and their five-year-old daughter, Sarah. Ms. Molloy-Williams was so distraught, that she broke into their home and left town with the kids. They changed their names to Jones and moved from one town to another for many years.

"I had to get the kids," Molloy-Williams testified. "I couldn't let that bastard get his hands on them."

She insisted that she did what she had to do to protect them from her abusive ex-husband.

"I had to do it. I was scared. I didn't know what he would do."

She testified that she feared for her life and her children's lives living with Seth Molloy. She was afraid of him.

"When he got drunk, he'd turn into a monster," she said. "He screamed bloody murder and threw things. He beat Robby so hard that there was blood all over the place."

Molloy convinced her not to report the incidents to the police because no one would believe her. At the time, he was a respected defense attorney in the Townsend area.

During the divorce proceedings, he painted her as a lush, Molloy-Williams testified. She admitted lying about her injuries due to being accident prone. She told a doctor that she tripped and fell down the steps. He was never called as a witness.

"We lived in fear of his every movement, when he had a few drinks," Molloy-Williams testified. "It was like walking on eggshells...I feared for their lives."

When jurors reviewed evidence, they voted not guilty and her charges were dropped.

Molloy was bludgeoned to death four months ago. His second wife, Debbie, discovered his body about 9 p.m.

Monday April 21st. Robert (a.k.a. Adam Jones) was seen fleeing the premises at the time of his murder. He admitted sending his father death threats, and faces terroristic threat charges. His sister, Sarah (a.k.a. Yvonne), and girlfriend, Maggie Albright, have been accused of similar charges. In June, the women were arrested for allegedly making crank calls with the music of 'American Pie' playing in the background. The lyrics had been changed to *Today'll be the day that you die.*

Peter Molloy, 16, Seth's son from his second marriage, has been charged with voluntary manslaughter for hitting his father on the head with a poker. His trial is set for October.

Five years ago, Amelia "Lynn Jones" Molloy married psychiatrist Karl Williams, M.D. and settled in Arlington, Va.

Lynn finished reading the article and wiped tears from her eyes. She hugged Donald Jenkins and said, "I don't know how to thank you."

"You were very brave to do what you did, Mrs. Williams," he said. "We're not out of the woods yet, though. We still need to work on getting the felony charges dropped on your kids and Maggie Albright."

Karl took her hand and said, "Come on, we need a break." He shook Jenkins's hand and helped her into the S.U.V. Instead of heading to the beach, they made a slight change of plans first.

Karl opened the back door and Thomas Smith pulled his left leg out, then his right. He dangled them out of the S.U.V. door, working up his strength to get out. Karl reached for his hand and gave a gentle tug. Thomas stumbled to his feet and leaned toward his son-in-law. Lynn and Karl stood on either side of him as they approached the cemetery.

"I can do this," Thomas muttered as they slowly approached the gate. He refused to use his walker.

He pressed his weight on their shoulders as they reached Rose's tombstone. When they got to about five feet from it, he sank to his knees with their help, and placed a bouquet of tulips in front of her marker. Lynn wiped grass off the grave and gently patted her father's shoulder.

"I told you Amelia would come with me someday," Thomas said. "Here she is, my love."

Tears trickled down her cheeks. "I only wish I could have come sooner."

He reached for her hand and said, "You're here now."

"I'm sorry I haven't been around, Mom. I was so scared...the kids grew up just fine. But–they're in trouble with the law right now, but I'm sure you know."

Karl stood at a distance and watched. Thomas and Lynn talked quietly for a few minutes. When he was ready to leave, Karl helped the old man to his feet and they headed slowly back to the parking lot.

Raymond Sinclair folded the newspaper and laid it on the coffee table. Everyone's lives had been affected in so many ways by the horrible things that Seth Molloy did. It was time for picking up the broken pieces of their shattered lives. Before he could be there for them, there was one thing he had to do for himself. He knew that if he was ever going to have a chance with Debbie, he needed to straighten up his act.

He went into the church and sat in back. He got there late so he didn't have to talk to anybody. The room was packed. A businessman stood at a podium and talked about his downfall into a world of uncontrollable gambling. His love of playing the slots cost him his wife and family and his life's savings. He was penniless and now lived in a shelter. About an hour later, Raymond was profoundly moved by the stories these brave men and women shared.

Afterward, the leader of the group introduced himself. When the group left, he stayed to talk to Raymond as long as was necessary.

"I lost big time at the tracks and had to use my company's money to repay the debt..." he said.

Logan tossed the newspaper on his desk and glanced over at Joe Flosky.

"Molloy's gone, but do you think that's going to help these people?"

Joe shook his head and grunted. "They've gotta carry on with their lives and live in shame 'cause everybody knows."

"It's amazing to what lengths people will go to cover for each other."

"Isn't it though?"

"Secrets don't stay secrets forever."

"You're right."

Logan looked at the clock on the wall. It was about three o'clock.

"It's nice out. How about we call it quits for the day and go fishing?"

Joe grinned and said, "Sounds good to me."

They whistled on their way out of the building.

* * *

CHAPTER 28

Frank reeled in a trout and said, "So that's how I figured it out Gramps."

"It's a mighty shame the way the world's getting to be. A mighty shame."

"Molloy ruined a lot of lives. Can you believe he pushed his own daughter down the steps?"

He grimaced and said, "I don't even want to think about it."

By the end of the afternoon, they caught a bucket full of fish. Then they packed up and headed back to the retirement community. Gramps watched the rolling meadows slip by and would cherish his weekend with his grandson.

Frank pulled into the parking lot and helped Gramps out of the car.

"Frank, it's time you patched things up with Penny."

"Well–"

Gramps tapped Frank's face and said, "Don't make excuses. Things have ways of working out. Just call her and tell her you love her and—"

* * *

Frank arrived home an hour later and checked his mail. He went into the kitchen and noticed the answering machine was beeping. There were three messages. Her voice was on the third one: "Frank, I need to talk to you."

He reluctantly dialed her number and felt his voice rise when she picked up.

"Penny, I love you. I need to talk to you. We need to talk."

Frank stood in front of the Jaded Dragon Restaurant, waiting. Every so often, he looked out at the parking lot, then checked traffic on the highway. He saw a red Toyota approaching, and waited in anticipation. It got closer, but it wasn't her car.

"She won't show up," he muttered.

Five minutes later, he saw her pull into the parking lot. She got out and they hugged each other. Then he kissed her.

He stumbled over his words before his composure set in. "I'm sorry for the things I said. We can make this work. We need to talk about things."

She smiled and put her hand in his as they headed into the restaurant.

* * *

ACKNOWLEDGMENTS

I hope you enjoyed *Secrets Can Kill*. I just want to mention a few people who helped me get the book printed.

For many years, my mom and dad have read the first copies of everything I have ever written. They have spent many hours proofreading various versions of this book when it was in notebooks, as with other ones I have worked on. I appreciate your help and suggestions. I also want to express my gratitude to my friends and family for their constant support.

I want to thank Maribeth Fischer and the members of the Rehoboth Beach Writer's Guild for their support and encouragement to write things outside my comfort zone. I also want to thank Steve Robison and Terry McAnally for telling RBWG members about CreateSpace.

Once again, I want to thank LuAnn Smith for our after church talks about crime and legal business. I also want to thank Don DeGraff for our writing chats. They're a lot of fun.

I especially want to thank the staff of CreateSpace for helping me get this book off the ground, and for all their assistance during the book production.